JOSEPH - A RASTA REGGAE FABLE

D1521277

Barbara Makeda Blake-Hannah

JAMAICA MEDIA PRODUCTIONS LTD.
P.O.. BOX 727, KINGSTON 6, JAMAICA

Books by Barbara Makeda Blake Hannah

- Rastafari – The New Creation
- Home – The First School
- Growing Out – Black Hair & Black Pride

First Published: Jamaica Media Productions Ltd., 1991
2nd Edition: MacMillan Caribbean (2005)
3rd Edition: Jamaica Media Productions Ltd. 2013

For further information please contact:
Jamaica Media Productions Ltd.,
P.O. Box 727, Kingston 6, Jamaica.
E-mail: jamediapro@hotmail.com

Inspired by Jamaica in the Rasta Reggae Seventies.
In memory of a dream that could have been ...
... should have been.

CONTENTS

Typesetting: Tina True

PROLOGUE

"Life is just a series of fuckery trips, and I'm sorry I agreed to travel THIS trip. Roll up the god-damned windows and turn off the blasted radio."

With a right screw face, Ashanti folded her arms heavily across her chest and slumped down on the car seat. Beside the car on both sides, a line of people watched and cheered the procession of cars that stretched a mile behind them, and a few chains in front, the funeral cortege that was a victory march.

"I can't stand to see them. Yesterday, they never knew him, they couldn't find nothing to say about him. Today, everybody going on like he was their brother."

"He was that, in truth, Sister Shanty."

In the front seat Red Dread turned his head slowly, supporting the great weight of his locks wedged into a crown-shaped, white knitted tam covered with emblems of the religious-cultured movement for which Jamaica was most famous. Reluctantly, he reached out to the end the unceasing flow of music sung and performed by the man whose fleshy remains the line of cars followed, to the cheers of the crowds lining the roads.

"They never knew him," Ashanti huffed, scowling at the grinning faces and waving arms which stared at them for mile after mile. "If they had known him, they would have known who and what he was. They would have treated him better."

Red Dread, Mikey, and Sister Shaya considered this in silence, each of them turning over thoughts almost visibly in silence.
"He was the Psalmist, David, who gave us the songs and prayers, the laments, and the direction," said Mickey.

"He was St. John, the beloved disciple, who delivered Christ's message, and showed us the future paradise," said Red Dread.

Sister Shaya drew long on her spliff. Then with the smoke and

7

breath the emerged, said: "He was Christ of our times, for our times."

Ashanti's scowl slowly softened, then she laughed a low laugh, like a gurgle.

"His story should be told. The true story. Oh, I know the white rasta/ reggae, rip-off writers will rush to publish their bib bucks books; but how much can they tell of what it was really like, those whose history and race exclude them from a true understanding of what he really gave to to the heart and guts of Black people...yu know? A Jamaican should tell the story, someone who knew him, knew his life."

The car travelled for a few corners, then Red Dread said: "You should make it your duty, Sister Shanty."

"Me! I am not a writer. It would need a writer."

Ashanti's shock was real; she recoiled form the suggestion. But Red Dread insisted.

"What is a writer, but one used by the Father JAH to bring forth word? In the beginning was the Word, and the Word was with him, so since words come from Him, ask Him for them. Please, Sis. You have the education we never had, you went to secondary school." His eyes were pleading.

"We will help you remember. Ask Jah. We will ask with you.
Now. The four of us represent North, South, East and West. We will chant to the four corners, and ask the Father to give us the words."

They pulled the Morris Oxford taxi car over to the roadside, not caring that people had to move aside off the grassy banking to give them pass, and then walked and walked through the countryside, not knowing where, but knowing they would know when to stop, until the four of them sensed at the same time that this quiet shady spot under a grove of pine trees, was the place.

They looked at each other, peering deep into eyes to see in them a confidence, comfort and divine love, and they each turned outwards to face the points of the compass, while Red Dread, facing east, took a deep breath and expelled it in the Nyabingi warrior cry of praise.

They did not know that at that very moment that the four of them united in prayer and chanted loud the name of

JAH! RASTAFARI!

... the coffin had at that exact moment arrived in front of its tomb in the small country village where Joseph had been born and where his mortal remains would rest for eternity.

CHAPTER ONE

"His foundation is in the Holy mountains. The Lord (JAH) loveth the gates of Zion more than all the dwellings of Jacob."
PSALM 87; Vs. 1-2

My name is Ashanti. My father called me that. Its on my Birth Certificate. I was born in Trelawny in 1948. My mother couldn't stand the hard life, and left us when I was 3, so my father came to Kingston to seek work. He was a farmer, but he could make clay pots, so when we came to Kingston he took us to live in a yard in West Kingston where the dwellings were made of zinc and old lumber. He had some friends who also made clay pots and they gave us room till Papa could build shelter for us. What little food we had, we shared with each other.

They called the area Dungle, for it was a dung hill made of garbage dumped there each day from homes where they had enough to throw away. Sometimes me and the other children would walk through the Dungle to the seaside, and if we were lucky, a fishing boat would be on the beach and they would throw a few sprats to us, which we would carry home for the big soup pot that burned in the big yard. It was a happy life.

My father was one of the first beard men, like his friends. They spoke a lot about Marcus Garvey and Ethiopia, and were always reading the Bible, those who could read. My father would send me to school, whenever we had money, "so that you can read Bible," he would say.

Later, when the politicians bulldozed the Dungle in 1958, we moved and went to live on Wareika Hill in Eastern Kingston, near to his friend Ras Jama and the Kings of Africa who taught my father to make the African drums of various sizes, until my father became a master at making drums. Wareika was a nicer place to live than Dungle, because there was no smell, and no John Crows looking at you with their beady eyes and beaks dripping with rotting flesh, but there were only macca trees on the hillside and we children had to walk far to get water, even though we were in sight of the beauty of Kingston and its harbour spread out before us.

JOSEPH · A RASTA REGGAE FABLE

It seemed natural that I should follow my father's ways and grow as a Rasta, for I loved my father. He was gentle and quiet and when I was small he would hug me and sing songs to me and hush me when I cried for hungry belly.

At Wareika, my father had more company, more friends. At nights, along with the Bible readings, we now had the music of drums, and the singing of harmonies by men gathered around night fires. Sometimes the bad men, the runaway criminals, would come down from the upper levels of the hills, and join in the reasoning and singing, and the oneness.

It was there that I met Joseph Planter in 1970. He and some brethren had come to Ras Jama's house to reason and smoke herb. My father called me to bring the good herb pan from under the bed, and when I asked him for my spliff, after he packed the chalice, he asked this young man Joseph to roll it for me. He rolled a smooth spliff with his pretty fingers, and licked it, looking sideways at me. Then he asked me if he should light it.

Facety! Everyone knows that you only light a woman's spliff if she is your woman, or you want her to be.

"Me a big woman to you, boy" I said. He laughed.
"Woman is woman, young or old. So what---you have a man?"

My father stretched out his hand for the spliff.
"Ashanti is yu sister, Joseph. And yu mother. Love her that way."

Joseph laughed. "It hard for me to love woman that way, Fada."

"You should try to learn – make you able to love and be loved by many more women." My father was serious. Joseph's eyes opened up with what was clearly a bright thought. I took my spliff and lit it with a stick from the fire between the men and smoked it, enjoying it, as if I didn't notice how hard Joseph was looking at me. And then looking into himself.

11

Later, when the herb reached them and the reasoning had quieted down, Joseph started up a Rasta chant, low, slow, and while the elders took up harmonies, Joseph sang his clear voice above the sweet harmonies and drums, into the clear night's stars and silence.

It made me pay attention then. He saw me looking at him, and smiled. Later when he was leaving, he smiled and said "Peace and Love, Sister Shanty."

That's what he called me after that, Sister Shanty. And everyone calls me Shanty now, because of Joseph. They think the name comes from the shanty town where I live, but it's from Joseph.

*   *   *

It was Boxing Day before I saw Joseph again. The youth club on the Hill was keeping a Christmas treat for the poor people's children, and the children on the Hill were in a frenzy. They all wanted to go, but their parents didn't want to send them and show their poverty by doing so, despite the curry goat we could all smell cooking on a big wood fire behind the club house.

On the other hand, all the adults wanted their children to enjoy themselves at someone else's expense, and free themselves for the afternoon and evening, so the most they could do was threaten any bad behaviour with the punishment of not being allowed to go to the party.

It had been an exciting day. From early morning the schoolyard had been swept clean by the youths with lignum vitae branches which raised the dust in swirls around their barefoot legs. Then the broke-down sticks of desks and chairs on which the school children sat for lessons in the term time (JAH knows how so many children sat on so few pieces)-- were moved outside carefully so as not to damage them further, and the school room that doubled as a clubhouse for the youths at night was swept and mopped with water carried by the young girls of the Club, with their parents watching and asking how come they didn't do these t'ings at home, and everyone laughing.

"I don't know why we don't just finish mash up these things they call desks for the pickney to sit on," one of the youths said.

"Look at this bench," said another "one foot bruk off... the seat full-a splinter..."

"And the pickney have-fi glad fi get a seat on dem kinda thing... is a disgrace."

They all agreed, but still, they were careful, tender in their work.

Then the goat had been slaughtered by two elder dreads, whose reward was the prized skin, and then sent off to a nearby house to be cut up while the fire was built and the big pot made ready by being caked on the outside with mud to make washing easier afterwards. With the help of an uptown girl who came each week to help out the youth club, rice, cake and drinks had been begged from nearby merchants, and the youths were proud that – no matter how little – they had enough o be feeding children worse off than themselves.

There was Cherry – just delivered of twins four months ago, and she only 16. And Paul, not 'mad', at the moment, but lack daily nourishment and too much ganja was going to make him 'sick' again. Here was Bunny Dread – I wonder where he left the rest of his gunman friends.

All of them looking like the angels guarding Christ's manger. To tell the truth, maybe they WERE angels – at least for today. It's just the hill that made them angry, frustrated and wicked.

Our house was near enough to the clubhouse for me to watch the day's happenings. I saw when the Member of Parliament came in, going on like he owned the place, when the truth was that this was his first ever – and maybe his last visit, to Wareika Hill.

Surrounded by his badmen bodyguards, he looked like a fat red snapper flopping on the beach. When he ran out of people to say hello to, and got tired of people asking him for favours and money, he got into his car and – with a flash of dust in everyone's faces, left us on our own with our own. The breeze blew fresher and cooler then, and the bar on the corner by the clubhouse turned up it's reggae music.

I heard them playing an old time rudie song, just as the night began to make shadows, and saw a small crowd making happy actions around the bar front. I could see Joseph then, in the middle of them, looking proud with a silent smile on his face, for it was his hit song they were playing.

I tied up my locks and put on a fresh blouse, and walked over to the party, just as Joseph and his posse came on the scene. I was busy for awhile, looking for my sister's children and then brushing some of the dirt off them both before I got them a big plate of curried goat and whit rice and sat down to make sure they didn't fight over it.

"Me like see a woman take care of her youths."
The voice was over my shoulder and it was Joseph. I didn't correct his mistake.

"Only those two you have? Mek me give you a strong Rasta son."

He laughed and drew on his spliff, pointing his head in the sky and drawing the spliff from the bottom.

"Cho – is all you think about?" I turned to him.

"Sister Shanty! I didn't know it was you. Is jus' through I always check for Rasta daughters, but is jus' me likkle joke. No min' me. Come, mek me help you."

And surprisingly, the children stopped their fussing and kicking when he sat beside them. They looked up seriously into Joseph's face and listened as he told them they must be good because JAH loves little children, and that they must love righteousness and know themselves as Black Gods and Goddesses. Well, my sister does not see Rasta, and she doesn't tell the children of JAH, so it was the first time they had been spoken to like that, so soft and serious, but gentle. They just listened and listened.

We stayed at the party until late. The moon came out and made everything clear and bright. The shacks on the hillside looked peaceful and full of calm, the dogs barked in the night and the sound of blues dances mixed with the music coming from our sound system and made everyone aware that the night was a happy one.

Later, when my sister had come for the children and we all sat on the side of the session, talking, I asked Joseph: "How come you over this side of town tonight. Boxing Day is spree night. How come you nah spree?"

"My spree days could be over."

"Sounds like bad news."

"No, could be good," Joseph continued. "A white boy from a record company wants me to sign a contract with them."
"But that's great!" I was glad, but surprised that Joseph was not more enthusiastic.

"That can't be bad."

"That's what you think." Joseph was serious. "I sign so many contract with so many crooks, that I don't want to sign no more papers. All them man do is take my music and make money with it, and don't pay me. Every night me and the pickney them go bed hungry, and yet my record is so popular that the people-them a flock me."

"But a foreign company nah cheat you? I asked

"Ah-oh! You think white man not wickeder than black man? Is him teach black man to wicked. Still, is a company that check for Jamdown music. An' they sign some friends of mine. Tony Franklin with them. Is really Ras Jama I come to reason with, to see what he say 'bout it. If he says yes, I will sign. Come we go check Ras Jama."

We walked across the dirt and macca hillside, followed by Joseph's posse. Dreadlocks all, bad as hell, you could see it. Joseph's dreadlocks were just beginning to grow spiky from his head, like the macca.

Ras Jama's yard was filling up with parents who had collected their children from the party and put them to bed. The drums were beating a steady rhythm and every now and then a brethren would take up a kette drum and lick some sharp finger licks in a gallop. Two sisters dressed in long African robs were dancing that special Rasta dance – a jump on the spot with syncopated hops. They were not showing off, but simply adding to the music the best and only way they could, with their bodies.

A portion of herb came to our corner, the Joseph posse cut it up and rolled their big ital spliffs. Joseph's spliff was perfect; it was his trademark, a perfectly-rolled spliff made with the elegant fingers that women would soon admire and men envy for their expertise on the guitar.

Soon Ras Jama handed his drum to an elder dread, and came over to our group.

"Peace and Love, Brother Joseph. How the I?"

"Blessings, Father," Joseph bowed his head quickly in acknowledgment of a respected elder. "I come look some guidance from the I."

Carefully he told Ras Jama the details of the record company's offer. Ras Jama listened. Then he spoke about his recording experiences, when he cut the 6-side album "Mystic Revelation of Rastafari."

The record had been the first ever recording of Rasta music and culture and was distributed all over the world. From its popularity, it would seem that millions of copies had been sold.

"Look around you, Brother Joseph. Does this look like the home of a man whose music has traveled the world?"

Joseph looked around him. A two-roomed house, barely painted in red, gold and green, the hopeful steel and block shell of a structure adjoining, over which a grand sign "Cultural Centre and Library" had been painted. Ambition mocking despair.

Staring up into Joseph's face were the men who had made the music, created it in their souls from the echoes of their African ancestry, and poured it out of their fingers and mouths and instruments of brass, skin and string. Here were these men, united in their poverty, in the struggle to find daily bread, in blistered families, the children crying in the night for hunger, and above all – the constant fear and worry that the one pleasure that relieved their misery, the herb they smoked, was liable to cause them arrest, beating and imprisonment. The herb, AND the faith Joseph and every man there – locksed or unlocksed, openly or quietly professing – was a believer in

RASTAFARI!

"A record contract don't make you rich, Joseph." said Ras Jama.

"I know that, and if I didn't I can see it with my own eyes here in front of me." Joseph was serious.

"But is a decision you have to make yourself," Ras Jama continued. "Like buying racehorse. Don't let any man tell you what to buy. Pick yourself. That way, if you win or lose, you can love or hate only yourself. JAH GUIDE."

And he turned and went back to the group of players, where a brother shifted off the kette drum and Ras Jama slid onto his stool, and in a second looked like he and the stool and the drum were one, had always been one, and would always be till Kingdom come, when he would be seen licking the same plik-plik lick on the little kette drum, beside the throne of JAH.

*　*　*

In London, the man called "Busha" stirred in his bed. Beneath his pale but handsome body, soothed the softness of a vicuna blanket. In the centrally-heated room, a green plush carpet and potted palm trees gave an impression of the tropics. Adding to the tropical setting was the golden-bodied woman who slept beside him. He lifted his arm, on which she lay and she stirred, opened her eyes and smiled at his smile.

"Time to get up, if you're to catch your plane."

A small frown crossed her forehead beneath the golden brown ringlets that advertised her part-European ancestry.

Zueleika's beauty was not only of the face and form, but especially of colouring. St. Elizabeth nayga, we called them. She was a world-famous singer now, part of a male-female duo which Busha had discovered in a West Indian club near Paddington singing for her rent money. Her partner, a black Jamaican, had been her lover at the time, but was soon replaced by Busha, who was so far her longest and most enduring lover.

At the time Busha had merely been a rich Jamaican-white boy trying to make a living selling the music he liked to dance to – much to the dismay of his very aristocratic family, who felt that such music was only suitable for maids and gardeners. Now, Busha was head of Tropic Records, a millionaire and lover of good life. He knew how to live like a playboy – homes in London, Paris, New York and the Bahamas, not to mention several in Jamaica where his ancestors had inherited land given to them for the purpose of slave-labour sugar.

She, Zuelika, was of dirt-poor Jamaican peasant stock, saved only from a miserable existence by her skin and hair colour – both the palest brown. Her German ancestors had carefully preserved the highly prized attributes of colour, but it was JAH himself who had given her her beauty.

Marriage between them was unthinkable, but as lovers they were complete, they had an understanding that transcended the frequent affairs they each had with other partners. He liked her because she was full of laughter and happiness, naturally, and fun to have around. The only thing she took seriously was her work, and she fully intended to have a Grammy on her mantlepiece one day.

Busha found her beauty a great prize, fit only for a king such as himself. A Grammy would be good, so he nurtured her career and their affair. Both were important to his financial well-being.

"Suppose he doesn't like me?"
A small frown crossed her forehead.

"It's up to you to make him like you," Busha answered with a small slap which rolled them both out of bed.

"The contract includes your two percent. But he WILL sign. He knows that I am the best that ever happened to him. I'm giving him any amount of money he needs to make an album. No one has ever offered him that before. He's great! His music drives the dancers wild with freedom. I HAVE to have him! He's the best thing that happened to ME.

"So get your sweet ass down there and make sure we have him signed by New Year's Day. I'd go, but he's afraid of "de white man" and he made a face which made her laugh.

*   *   *

And also in London, in an office overlooking the Thames Embankment, a man put down a newspaper, picked up a phone and said: : "Bring me a file on the Rastafari cult."

CHAPTER TWO

"Listen, O isles, unto me; and hearken, ye people, from far. The Lord (JAH) hath called me from the womb; from the bowels of my mother hath he made mention of my name. And said unto me, Thou art my servant, O Israel, in whom I will be glorified.
ISAIAH, Chapter 49; Vs. 1,3.

Zuelika stretched her arms lazily above her head and looked out towards the mountains of St. Andrew, from her room on the 10th floor of the Kingston Sheraton Hotel. Before her, seemingly within fingertip reach, stretched the horizon-wide view of the luxury homes dotting the upper reaches of the St. Andrew Blue Mountain Peak which she could see far in the distance of the clear blue sky.

Nothing gave her a greater feeling of having 'made it', than to be here in her home country Jamaica, on top of the world. The suites of Paris' George Cinq, London's Dorchester and New York's Plaza -- hotels in which she had stayed with one or other of her rich and famous boyfriends -- seemed like cheap motels, compared with the attractive but simple furnishings of this room in the capital of her home country, Jamaica.

It was her first trip to Jamaica since leaving it nine years ago to seek 'fame and fortune' in England, with nothing more than Twelve Pounds in her pocket and her greatest asset – her looks. She had promised herself never to come back to Jamaica until she had 'made it' – a promise she had kept until today. Granted, there had been no photographers at the airport, nor television interviewers pounding on her door for an exclusive. But somehow, being in Jamaica as Tropic Records' representative gave her a feeling of power and achievement which surpassed any thing in her life so far.

She turned and flopped down on the large bed, her eyes looking around the room to make sure that everything was right for her forthcoming meeting. The basket of fruit, the music magazines on the bedside tables, the portable cassette player, and her briefcase, had all been laid out to impress her visitor with her wealth, importance and efficiency. But she had not left anything to chance, and the pleasant smell of Dior's *Diorissima* perfume still lingered in the air from the spraying she had just given the room.

Beside the briefcase lay her passport. She got up and replaced it in her briefcase. It would not do for her visitor to see that 'Zuelika' was in truth Opal Williams – the name her parents had given her at birth in the small village of German Town, St. Elizabeth.

No, that life was firmly buried in her past, and only a name in a passport served to remind her of the dirt roads, the kerosene lamp nights and the barefoot life she had lived as a child and endured until the age of sixteen. Then one night she had packed her few clothes into a bag, wished her peasant farmer parents a silent goodbye, and crept out the house. She hid in the bushes by the roadside until early morning to catch the market truck to Kingston, wedged between two fat women whose sizes protected her from the cold breeze, dust and discomfort of the long ride to Kingston.

She tried not to remember the man who introduced himself to her, as she stood amid the banana trash at the bus terminus at Parade, Kingston, trying to decide what she should do and where she could go, and offered to take her to "a nice boarding house". She had willingly gone with him, trustingly as only a semi-literate country girl could, and when she found that he not only expected her to share her room and have sex with heim, but also allow other men to do the same for money, she quietly resigned herself to her condition with the thought that as soon as she could she would leave.

The first brown-skinned man who returned a second time to savour her favours, was overjoyed to hear her confess her 'love' for him, and was only too glad to move her into a half of a house in Vineyard Town which he owned specifically for the purpose of accommodating his extra-marital affairs. He was a good provider; in the eighteen months she stayed there she acquired furniture, clothes, some good pieces of gold jewellery, and familiarity with the entertainment spots of the city.

One night at the Glass Bucket – Kingston's leading night club – she begged her boyfriend's permission to enter the amateur talent contest held there each week, and to the backing of Carlos Malcolm's Afro Jamaica Rhythms, sang a good version of *"Tears On My Pillow"* and won the event. After that, she was determined to make a career as a singer especially because she saw that her combination of European features and roots Jamaican manners, made her stand out from the crowd and made the men in the audience applaud her performance much more than her talent deserved.

When her lover's irate wife finally found out about her and visited the Vineyard Town house to curse her as loudly and crudely as possible from the sidewalk, she knew that it was only a matter of time before her past caught up with her in the small Kingston society. She went to a jeweller, sold her gold pieces, and bought her plane ticket to London.

London was full of West Indians who had come there in the first wave of immigration in the late 50's. In 1963, the year of Zuelika's arrival, the white population of Britain was just beginning to make felt their racist anger at having to live and work with Black people, and for a time Zuelika passed as "white," working as a waitress in little restaurants, or a salesclerk in shops. But her accent and style still marked her as 'foreign' and she soon gave up pretending to be other than she was – a Jamaican. This she found, could be turned to advantage if she chose the right avenues.

So she looked for another "Glass Bucket" and found versions of it in the various small basement clubs which had opened up in the Black ghettos of London to serve the West Indian community's need to relax far from the real, racist world outside. Brixton, Peckham, Ladbroke Grove and Paddington came to know Zuelika, (the name she adopted after seeing if on the cover of a book an upper-class-looking girl was reading beside her on the bus).

She had learned in her young life so far, that a beautiful woman without a man around her was easy prey for all the hustlers, con-men and pimps – black and white – who abounded in the world, so she chose a man again to keep her company and help her career. Men in England were either black or white – no in-between browns – so this time she chose a black Jamaican, 'Spinner' – a young Brixton market trader who also had ambitions as a singer.

They became a duo, singing versions of the Blue Beat songs that were coming out of Jamaica to the grateful welcome of the music-starved West Indian population, and it was there that Busha had found her, trained her, romanced her, and given her the chance to improve her speech and style until her Jamaican origins were well disguised beneath the exterior of beauty and fashion.

It had all been so easy, Zuelika reflected, flinging her long hair off her shoulders in a familiar gesture of freedom. Opal was dead. Now, only Zuelika lived.

The ringing of the telephone put an end to her thoughts.

"I am here," a rough voice said.

"Come on up. Room 1207," and she took one last look at her reflection in the mirror.

Zuelika was totally unprepared for the sight that greeted her when she opened the door. Outside stood three men who looked as if they were street robbers who had entered the hotel unnoticed. They each wore dirty, broken football shoes, trousers that should have been washed long ago, and T-shirts which drooped and sagged from much wear and tear. All three had dreadlocks hanging down from beneath discoloured knitted tams, the ends of the knotted hair bunching and springing this way and that without any apparent concern of their wearers.

But it was their eyes that made Zuelika frightened to the pit of her stomach.

They were hard and angry, watchful and resentful, like men about to enter a boxing ring in a fight they were determined to win. All the street cunning that Zuelika had learned over the years; came to her rescue, and her mouth went into automatic drive just as quickly as her mind raced to cope with the situation.

"Aha!" she said brightly. "Come in. Which one of you is Joseph?"

The shortest and the least handsome of the three said grudgingly: "I."

"Come. Let's sit on the terrace and talk."

Picking up the fruit basket, Zuelika led the way to the balcony overlooking the hotel's pool, and sat down.

"What would you like? A banana? Starapple? How about some grapes?"

"Peel some for us," ordered the tallest of the trio, in a voice that waited for refusal.

"Ha, ha, ha," Zuelika laughed, picking out a bunch of fat purple grapes.

That son of a bitch, she thought. Who does he think I am – his wife? But cool, Zuelika girl, you've peeled grapes for guys before, under more pleasant circumstances. So no big thing now for these barbarians, if that is what it takes to get them 'soft'.

Slowly, with the elegant fingers and pointed nails that were also part of her beauty, she peeled the skin off three grapes, as they watched in silence. By the third grape, Zuelika saw that her senusal powers had taken charge of the situation. The three were fascinated by her actions, and the peeling of each grape was watched as intently and with as much fascination as if it had been her clothes she was peeling off. She uncrossed her legs, knowing that more of her thigh would be revealed, and pretending she did not notice.

Then she used one free hand to fling her hair over her back in her usual gesture, and with a sweet smile she offered the grapes one apiece to each man, beginning with Joseph.

As Joseph put his grape in his mouth, she took another from the bunch, peeled off its skin, placed it in the centre of her puckered lips, and slowly sucked it into her mouth.

Then, with a sweet smile, she said: "more?"

And when they shook their heads, unable to answer in voices, smiled again and said: " Shall we get down to business?"

Without taking his eyes off her, Joseph gestured to the other two.

"Mickey. .. Tension. Go downstairs and see if they sell carrot juice in this Babylon place." Then without looking at their departure, he slung one leg over the arm of his chair, took a spliff out his pocket and lit it, inhaling the smoke while the door closed.

Joseph looked Zuelika over from head to foot, and then up again. Noting his interest, Zuelika got and walked slowly inside the room to get her briefcase, knowing that her every move was being watched by Joseph.

"So is you Busha sen'." said Joseph on her return. "The man is rude to sen' a woman to do a man's job."

"Nothing is a man's work anymore," Zuelika replied with another large smile.

"I am the person Busha most trusts to handle his most important business."

She waited a while, to see if Joseph would understand the true closeness of her relationship with Busha, and watched to see his reaction. By the tightening of his lips, she assumed that he understood, but was not pleased.

"Mek me see the contract," was all he said.

She handed over the papers, but he simply glanced at them, leafing over the pages without really reading them.

"Me have fi mek somebody else read these – mek sure you people not cheating me, like all the others."

Zuelika smiled again and pulled out her top card.

"The contract guarantees you Ten Thousand Dollars for recording costs over three months, another Ten Thousand for living expenses during that time, and a 5 percent royalty on all sales after the production and promotion costs are deducted."

"A so much money? Is buy him a-buy me like race horse? What him expect to get after him spen' all that money?"

"He wants one album in the first six months, with an option for two more in the following eighteen months. He thinks that with the kind of promotion he plans for you and the group, the public will want to hear more as soon as the first album is out. That's why he is paying out so much more to make this first album really great. He wants you to use the best studio, and to have everything you need, so you can concentrate on making music, instead of worrying about how you are going to pay your domestic bills. Frankly, he wants to make you a STAR."

Joseph dismissed this last statement angrily. "Me a STAR a' ready. Me no need him to mek me into no star again."

Oops. Zuelika realized that she had said too much, perhaps destroyed the good she had already stacked up in her favour. She smiled again, and leaned forward to touch the papers in Joseph's hand, knowing full well that he would look at her breasts swelling under the Indian cotton blouse.

Then she said: "Take the papers with you, and read them. Then call me and we'll talk again. I'll be here for three days, and I need your answer by then."

She got up indicating that the meeting was over, for she heard sounds outside the door that Joseph's two brethren had returned.

"Happy New Year, in advance," she said as she opened the door, and watched as they departed, Tension muttering: " No bumboclaat carrot juice in the blouse-and-skirt hotel..." but she noted that Joseph turned and looked back at her before he entered the lift, and his face was no longer angry, but calm, even happy.

Now wait, she thought and ordered a bottle of Chablis. After all, it was New Year's Eve and since she had to spend it alone, she might as well get drunk.

It was the next evening, before Joseph called her. In that time, Zuelika had lots of time to consider the previous day's meeting. And Joseph himself. And she had arrived at the conclusion that she would like this man to fall in love with her... this man from her former world, the world before her fame and flashbulbs, before the limousines, the caviar...and the abortions.

This man who had not let go one ounce of his Jamaican-ness, this man who she was going to make into a superstar. She found him the most exciting man she had ever met, and she kept thinking what it would be like to feel his locks falling on her naked body as they made love.

* * *

You know, this Rasta thing is a funny thing.
Rasta is good and Rasta is bad. Rasta is beautiful and Rasta is ugly. Rasta is madness, and Rasta is so much sense, that it makes some people glad and some people angry.

The people Rasta makes glad are the people like Joseph and me, and some of you. Rasta makes us glad, because it is the first story Black people ever heard that we are not the losers. It's the first time we got a good reason for having Black skin and wooly hair. The first time we ever heard good things about Africa and Africans.

27

Rasta is such a high spiritual heights, that if confounds the so-called wise, and is revealed only to those who some consider poor and stupid. It is a philosophy that appeals to the soul, for if it appealed to the brain, we would have to read it to understand it, and how many of us can read? So rasta is a soul understanding that brings Peace and Love when the Understanding/Overstanding is reached.

But it is a fire too: A fire to point to the wickedness of the world's way of life, to burn it with words. Burn it out of yourself, especially. The Holy Fire that burns away the trash from inside your life and leaves a clean field on which to plant some new crops, like when you plant tobacco you must burn the trash you clear off the land before you sow the seeds.

Rasta and Fire. In the fire you will see Rasta and see yourself, your I-self, your soul, your God. Selassie I, JAH, Christ in a new human form.

It was that livity we were living in 1972. Rasta was getting stronger, not so much fight from those above, those with power they had no intention of handing over to Rasta just because Rasta was right. So fight, they fought us, fought the fire. But the fight was getting weaker, because we were getting stronger. The fire was getting hotter.

* * *

The rattle of an old car, a screech of brakes and a lot of loud noises, informed me that Joseph was outside. My girlfriend Shaya and I were giving the house a good clean and tidy so the New Year would start fresh tomorrow. Our peas soup was on the fire, waiting for the yam and dumplings we were going to make as soon as we finished the last of the red polish on the floor. Our house was all wood, humble and small, but clean.

"We going to Cane River Falls to wash our locks," he said with great energy. "Come nuh?"

Yes, there could be no nicer way to fresh off the sweat and clean out the floor polish out of our fingernails. But the soup encouraged us to stay home.

"Bring it with you. Bring the coal stove too. We a-spend the night up there – bus' 1973 in Zion."

This needed a conference between myself and Shaya, but eventually we agreed that each was enough protection from love-starved dreads, so we agreed to the trip.

I knew it was important to Joseph that I come, because I knew that even if he didn't say so, he hadn't yet made up his mind about the contract and he felt the night would bring a sign if he watched and waited.

So, with a lot of disturbance, especially of the disapproving neighbour next door who was always watching our business, we re-adjusted the several dreads and youths traveling in the open-backed van, set the coal fire in a corner wedged between coconuts and green bananas, and set off with a variety of happy noises.

We reached the Falls about five o'clock, just as evening was beginning to lower her dark arms. We trod like young goats down the steep rock staircase that took us to the foot of the Falls, and with cries of joy, the assorted dreads rushed to the water, tearing off what little clothes they wore.

The cascade of water plunged fifty feet down over the lip of a big rock, water pounding to a crash below, where only the strongest and bravest dreads would stand under, letting it's mighty force beat down on locks and head and body. There were loud cries of bravery, shrieks of joy and lots of splashing from all, while we sisters found a stream of water which was not as fierce and attended to our own cleansing still wearing the T-shirts and slips we had stepped under the water with.

Bathing under your clothes is an art only gained by much practice of outdoor life, and we had much.

We shared a sweet-smelling shampoo with our brethren, and even our towels after we had finished using them, and sat on the top of a large smooth rock to dry our locks. One by one, the dreads of all ages found themselves each a rock of their own on which they sat and fanned their locks in the evening breeze.

A tarpaulin was spread across three sticks beside another rock, and a shelter was created beside which our pot and stove were placed and a fire started. As usual when dreads are present, we sisters did not have to cook, but instead allowed to rest as queens, and we delighted in time spent oiling our locks, smoothing cream into our legs and feet, wrapping ourselves in our robes and our locks with bright crowns, which we took our time to wind as creatively as we wished.

Then the food was ready, and we filled our 'bashes, ate and drank water from the river, and from the coconuts we had brought with us.

Then spliffs were built, and from each rock a curl of smoke marked the place where a man sat and meditated.

Soon the drums began to sound, a melody began, and then our songs started, with each dread taking turns from his rock to send up a chant, a sound, and a cry of triumph like the blowing of the final trumpet; sounds of the names of the Father JAH, some of the secret names known only to those who search for the hidden mysteries of the Life given to I&I.

The hymns "*Satta Amasagana*", the Nyabingi song, "*Africa We Want to Go*" and the song that Joseph was then best known for : "*I've Got A Right to My Sight of JAH*", were some of the songs that poured out of the crack in the mountain which we were using as our temple. The moon was in quarter and its light was as bright as that of a full moon. For a few hours, we were in a heaven of our own, undisturbed by the world outside.

As Joseph stood up on his rock and chanted the words of his defiant battle song, I saw in him what many would soon see and admire to the point of stardom. It was the defiant thrust of his chest like a rooster, head upward, in a pose that was one of direct contact with the Creator to receive electricity flowing back to him from the heavens, the earth and the air. When he sang like that, there was nothing else in the world but Joseph and JAH, and the energy that powered his body and soul was a river a river from which he drank as directly, as seriously, and as needfully as a baby on it's mother's titty.

It was that nearness to JAH that all who saw him sing, respected and wanted to be close to. Of COURSE he would sign the contract. He owed it to JAH to give the world this special gift.

*   *   *

Let me tell you a secret about Joseph. He did not think he was good looking. His illegitimate birth and pale skin marked him as the unwanted alliance of black poor and white flesh-user, and the taunts of his childhood when they called him "Eagle" because of his long thin nose, still haunted him. Only after his locks grew long, did he feel comfortable with his looks, and by then he was so past vanity, that his looks did not bother him at all.

So, as he later told me, he was amazed that this woman of the world Zueleika would find him attractive. Yet he had hoped she did, which was why he had chosen the time of their next meeting, and made sure that he was alone when he knocked at the door.

"Shall I peel you another grape?" she said jokingly, doing a mock Mae West drawl on her small joke: then seeing that he did not understand the joke she simply stepped out of her loose dress and let him look at the immense beauty of her body.

Making love with a Rastaman was not much different from any other man, except that his hair and his animal-ness made the experience even more exciting than usual.

She gave him the best of her sexual arts, and she knew that she surprised him with some tricks that he obviously knew nothing about, or never imagined that a woman knew about.

When they were finished, she suggested they take a bubble bath together, and when he did not understand what a bubble bath was, she delighted in introducing him to that special pleasure, soaping his body, making peaks and valleys in the foam, playing like children, and then being swept up in the passion of it so much that they barely had to time to wipe off the foam and water before falling on the floor in another sexual embrace.

Then she oiled his body with orange and rosemary oil, and played with his locks, handling them, twisting, plaiting and rolling them in her hands, until she had satisfied her curiosity.

"I am your first Rastaman?" was all Joseph said.
"Yes," she said. "My wild and wooly animal."
She caressed his locks.

"Let me be the first and the last," he urged.

Zuelika laughed. "Only if you sign the contract. Then you can have me, signed, sealed and delivered."

"It's a deal."

*   *   *   *

The effect Zuelika had on Joseph surprised him. Her sexual skills were of a variety he had never before experienced.

Joseph's sexual experience was identical to other youths and men of the ghetto poor. At an early age he had seen and heard the grunting couplings of his friends and neighbours, and when the urge had come upon him in early manhood, he sought out willing partners – girls who themselves sought out sex – and relieved himself of his needs.

Little love, tenderness or skill ever entered those couplings, not until he met Rosy, the 16-year-old whose family was loving enough to have taught the quiet young woman enough tenderness to make Joseph return again to the small bed she occupied on the back verandah of her parent's tiny house, and squeak the springs until silence and rest.

Perhaps it was the rest he felt in Rosy's arms that he called 'love', but it was enough to make him marry her when a year later she told him she was pregnant. His apprenticeship with the corner radiator shop did not pay enough to rent an apartment, but Joseph begged lumber and zinc and fixed up the shed at the back of the radiator yard into a small but clean room, where he, Rosy and the baby – a boy – lived.

It was not a great life, and the pressure of work and family often left Joseph to hang out more and more with his man friends, who did a lot of sidewalk sitting around the recording studio nearby, watching the comings and goings, and slowly but surely getting into the music world.

It was there on the corner Joseph had got hold of his first guitar, it was there that he first hammered out a tune and found some words to match, and it was there that he got his first chance to back up a leading singer's vocals with harmony on a record.

In such an environment, Joseph and his friends met girls and women, and took their sexual opportunities as they came – like most young men of their group. Fidelity to marriage vows was something that did not rest well with the natural attraction to women. But under all his experiences, the pull of Joseph's spiritual consciousness made him ask the question: "What is Love?"

He could answer the question when it referred to humanity, or the Creator, or to his child. But when it referred to woman, he could not yet say in his heart depths that he fully knew what it was.

Zuelika's entry into Joseph's life changed that. In months that followed, as he prepared the first Tropic album and for the first tour of England, Joseph found himself tossed like a small boat on a sea of turbulent love with Zuelika.

Zuelika was not like anyone Joseph had ever experienced. She settled into a large apartment Busha kept on the Jacks Hill Skyline overlooking Kingston, and made it a love nest for two.

The life she lived was fascinating. She thought nothing of renting a projector to screen a film for two, or of spending an entire day in bed making love.

She told Joseph to teach her everything about Rasta, and he was amazed to find that she knew nothing about Africa or the politics of Blackness. To Zuelika, Angela Davis was simply a girl with a cute new hairstyle.

She knew even less about God-JAH and in the moments when the volume of physical passion overwhelmed his consciousness, he would take up his Bible and read it to her, hoping to bring an understanding of righteousness that could make him fully love her. In so doing, he hoped to make a saint out of the sinner he was certain Zuelika must be, to have acquired so much sexual expertise.

As for Rosy, she was by now accustomed to his frequent absences for many days and nights while he and the brethren and musicians camped together at Nyabingi, or bunkered down to rehearse music, or just simply went on an island trod. Even if she suspected Joseph was with another woman, what could she do?

Nothing, except look after her child, cook what food Joseph had brought for them, or go over to her parents to ask for help when things ran out before Joseph returned.

She was glad about the Tropic contract – what she had heard of it, and now that Joseph was giving her money regularly, she was glad to rest with her child or visit one of her many girlfriends who spoke about hairstyles and clothes and other people's business – topics she could relate to much better than Joseph's Rasta reasonings.

The contrasts between Rosy and Zuelika was so great, Joseph marvelled. It made him wonder how the two could be of the same species – woman. One was quiet, hardly ever speaking an original thought, no opinions or experience of the world outside her neighbourhood, sexually modest to the point of boredom.

The other was a firebrand, a butterfly of thoughts and actions, and a sexual whirlwind. Her limitless horizons inspired him to reach farther in his musical creations. Her conversations and questions showed him what kind of lyrics people needed to hear. The people and places and events she told of, made him realise he could be as expressive as he dared.

Once he arrived home to find that she had placed candles throughout the house, and incense sticks, bowls of imported nuts, and flowers, while she was sitting on the carpeted floor naked except for a red chiffon scarf, reading aloud the Songs of Solomon.

On another occasion, the house was full of children she had collected in her jeep from the ghetto at the foot of the hill, and was treating to cake, ice cream, balloons and games, like a big happy sister. It was the mixture of sinner and saint that intrigued Joseph and kept him coming back for more. He was convinced he could rescue the Saint in Zuelika.

*   *   *   *

Joseph stared working with the Cubs to make the first music that allowed them to do whatever they wanted. No more quick-into-the-studio-for-one-take musics. Now he had all the time to build up his songs and lay the different instrumental tracks on the basic melody.

Busha issued instructions to his people in Kingston to move the Cubs into an old house which he had owned uptown, a house with several apartments which could house the musicians and give them rehearsal room, as well as living space. The Cubs moved in and stripped the interior bare of all it's contents, before they felt at home, moving in cushions, mats and hammocks as furniture, for the pride of lions that formed the retinue of this king.

On my first visit there with a bunch of bananas from my yard, I was amused but pleased to see to see this piece of the ghetto in the middle of the posh uptown neighbourhood. Some chickens scratched in the backyard, callaloo and okra had been planted in a bed at the fence, while a dread was up the ackee tree picking fruit, and another sitting on the kitchen step shelling peanuts for making peanut milk.

Upstairs, Joseph sat on the floor among some brethren, humming a tune and trying to fit words and chords to it. On the verandah, a table tennis match was in progress between Mikey and Small Youth. On the other side of the high bouganvillea hedge, I could hear a power motor almost drowning out the sound of some American pop music being played on an expensive hi-fi in the safe, secure, middle-class apartments next door.

I offered to help the dread in the kitchen prepare the callaloo, but with a smile he said: : "Joseph only like to eat from man." So I sat for a while, smoked a spliff, and went on to my next appointment.

* * * *

The tour of England to promote the album was a musical success, and a public relations blessing from the start for Tropic Records. The Lyceum Theatre in London's West End is an ugly building outside. But inside it is like a church dedicated to the performing arts, a miniature opera house covered in red velvet and soft lights illuminating the curves of seats.

Downstairs, the seats had been removed for Joseph and the Cubs show, and around the sloping floor prowled lions and cubs of all variety of race and fashion. There were fancily dressed hippies in long skirts, men with long hair and beards, smelling of patchoili oil.

There were the Skinheads, British bad boys delighted to be mixing shoulder to shoulder with the black kids they grew up with in the slums, who their parents had said they should not speak to, but who the defied by copying the short haircuts, tight pants and little hats worn by the black kids who had such good music coming from their council flats every day.

36

There were the black kids themselves, who had spread the word about "this amazing group that look like wooly savages, but play the best music to come out of Jay-A since Desmond Dekker..."

And there was the pride of the pack – a few dreadlocksed pioneers of the Rastafari movement – who stood casually but, oh so conscious of every stare, in groups around the hall or walked up and down the staircase of interested and excited people.

The opening act was Dekker himself, to the delight of the skinheads, who sang along with his every song and begged for more.

But when Joseph took the stage with a leap and, pointing to every man and women there, sang *"The Revolution Begins Right Now,"* it seemed that every hand was raised and every body strained to return back the energy, the joy, the strength and the pleasure of this man's musical communication.

He ranged through his entire repertoire that night; rocked them with *"Rock Me In Your Arms,"* provoked them with *"Shall We Smoke"* (which everyone took as a signal to light up a spliff), taught them with *"Africans Awake"* and *"Stepping Up To Zion."*
And above the lyrics was the good music, the hummable tunes and the dancing rhythms of reggae, happy music, music that reaches your soul, music of the Gods of Jamaica, highest outpost of Ethiopia.

Yes, after that night, he was made.
A superstar, a legend in his own time.
That night he forgot the bitter weather, the cold rooms, the bad food, the cold English people, and the sacrifices of his life.
That night he forgot all the pain.
From that night on, he knew only the Love of the Father, JAH.

When he tried to leave the stage, the crowd went wild.
After three encores, the police had to be called to get the audience to leave the theater.

Bathed in sweat in the small dressing room behind the stage, Joseph sat in numb silence as a hurricane of noise and people curled around him. People slapping him on the shoulders, people wiping the sweat from his face, people shouting at the mob, trying to open the door and come in to congratulate their star person. In all the commotion, Joseph was like a statue.

He brushed off Zuelika's kiss, though he was pleased, and looked at the people from Tropic Records, standing in their uniform of faded denim pretending to be nobodies, but knowing that everyone knew them, aware of their 'discovery' and the hit he had become, but not sure what to do until instructions came from Busha.

Some of the dreads from the audience had squeezed themselves into the dressing room, and stood smiling happily, locks pouring down from under multi-coloured crowns, smoking their giant cone spliffs openly in the crush and heat of it all. Four of them surrounded Joseph, still sitting cross-legged and silent, and talked to him seriously for a few moments in words that left him still serious, but more thoughtful.

Their farewell was almost a salute, as they left, the khaki of their clothes making them visible in the crowd until they could be seen no more.

And when the celebration finally died down, back at the small hotel in Earl's Court where they stayed, Zuelika insisted on time for herself, and took him on a tour of HER London, showing him off at the trendy nightclubs she frequented with her rich and famous friends, and in which he sat with loose locks and frayed denim among the fashionably dressed dancers, watching girls show themselves off for him, and men eye Zuelika as she sat beside him, feeding him pieces of raw vegetables and fruit from a bowl beside them.

And then to Covent Garden as dawn lighted, for onion soup which Joseph had never had but would henceforth delight in, even getting the recipe for Chef to make up in our Kingston kitchen.

And finally to bed. In luxury of the best sheets Knightsbridge sold, perfumed with Zuelika's special scent, she embraced him in love and gratitude.

*   *   *   *

And in the Office on the Embankment, the file was a little thicker the morning after the concert, as newspapers struggled to report on and interpret this new phenomenon on the musical, cultural and racial scene – Rasta/Reggae.

The man on the phone was saying: "...this thesis...sells out his Black brothers a bit overmuch, don't you think?... Oh, you call it critical analysis... we need to send someone who knows what he is doing... well, let's try him ... give him a cover, book commission, or something like that ... you know how to fix things up. And hear me ... No mistakes, you hear?"

*   *   *   *

The Lyceum show was the high spot of a tour that had been a boring trudge across the bleak English countryside, staying in cheap lodgings which were the only ones that would accept the 'wooly dreads', or else in parrafin-heated flats of Jamaicans in cities like Bristol, Birmingham and Manchester, where the children of the immigrant West Indians grew, suffering in hatred of racism – a hatred that made them appropriate candidates for the Gospel of Rastafari.

The tasteless English food, all seemingly made of artificial ingredients or pork, made Joseph and the Cubs sick. The polite racism of the English, the cold, the lack of light, and the distance from home, led to many irritations among the group.

The final straw was when they had a meeting with Tropic Records staff after the Lyceum show, to try and get some money to fulfill their dreams of buying a car, a stereo or a TV to take back home as proof of their financial success.

The Tropic Records staff all worked in one large room, decorated with soft cushions which formed a circle around a sunken glass-topped table, under which swam tropical fish. Their cool, laid-back manner irritated Joseph and the Cubs, and they sat down on the cushions with the attitude of people who knew a fight was about to begin.

"You owe US," said Tropic. And they produced a list of figures of public relations, promotions, drivers, stage managers, secretaries, etc... which did indeed look as if Joseph and the Cubs owed Tropic a fortune, some Eight Thousand English Pounds.

As they say, all hell broke loose. Zacky, the most mystic of the group, called Tropic "thieves and rogues" and stormed out in a thunder of noise, leaving them to JAH.

Tony "Tension" let loose a string of those Jamaican bad words which use to earn us Forty Shilling fines in the old days, and cursed them Nyabingi style.

"Onoo parasites and blood-sucking vultures! Onoo come to take away I kingdom, t'ief I gift from JAH, and tell I say I owe you money! You must be the original slave master pickney dem! The children of Satan, who must be sat-on by the Children of JAH. FIYA! BLOOD AND FIYA! Death and Destruction to all of you Annie Palmer Elizabeth children! Onoo pickney of Henry Morgan and John Hawkins! Onoo suck onoo mumma bumboclaat.! FIYA!

Joseph said he just sat silently through it all, but now, telling us gathered on the verandah of the old house, he hugged himself with laughter, as did we, seeing in our minds' eyes the scene with Tony shouting and cursing in the people's office.

"The Tropic people, dem quake. Them never get cuss by a Rastaman before. Them skrunch up in the cushions, and start back 'way, then one girl scream and Tension turn on her with him red eye-them bulging out, and she jump and run out of the room screaming for help.

"Some security man come in and go fi grab Tension, but him jump back and say: 'Touch not the Lord's annointed!' and them never hear that one before, so them jump back and Tension passed through them like Moses walking through the Red Sea, and we all just jump up and step behind him, and walk out."

We were laughing uncontrollably now, as Joseph recounted the scene.

"You can laugh now," said Joseph, as we subsided. "But that scene cost me my two best friends and my two best musicians. Joseph and the Cubs is no more. Wha' me-a-go-do?"

Yes, Tension and Zacky had left the Cubs, vowing never to work again for Tropic Records or tour with Joseph.

We were serious and silent now. We knew Joseph was thinking about how to form a new group, and we knew it wasn't easy, especially since the news about the split had left everyone mystified.

Plus, a new record was needed from Joseph, to fulfill his contract.

He needed somewhere to think, somewhere away from the young white journalists who had started flocking to Jamaica for interviews with him. There were so many of them – some sent by Tropic to further publicize Joseph, others who had come on their own – hearing about Joseph and Rasta and seeking the story of stories.

I sat and listened to one of these journalists interview Joseph. The man was nervous, because there were about seven of us in the room, and only him as a white man, and he soon realised it was HE who was being interviewed. But he felt confident because of who he was and the paper he represented, until little by little, like air coming out of a balloon, he came to realise how inferior he and his way of life was, to that of this ragged man sitting barefoot and bare-chested in a bare wooden room.

JOSEPH: *So what you want to know?*

REPORTER: *First of all, how do you get your hair like that? Do you put cow dung in it?*

JOSEPH: *(to us) Insult him a-insult me, you know. (to reporter) No I wash it and oil it just like you. I just don't comb it.*

REPORTER: *Why?*

JOSEPH: *Why not?*

REPORTER: *Tell me about Rasta. Do you have to be black to be Rasta?*

JOSEPH: *Yes, but plenty Black people can't be Rasta. And No, Rasta is not a skin colour.*

REPORTER: *Haile Selassie – wasn't he just a little tyrant who liked dressing up in uniforms and feeding his lions while his people starved?*

JOSEPH: *MOVE THIS BUMBOCLAAT MAN FROM MI HOUSE. MOVE HIM BEFORE I KILL HIM!*

By encounters like these, Joseph's name travelled the world, and the Philosophy of Rastafari began spreading beyond the ghettos and the Nyabingi, to the hearts and minds of a music-loving people.

CHAPTER THREE

" Oh come, let us sing unto the Lord (JAH); let us make a joyful noise to the rock of our salvation."
PSALM 95; V.1

People were still arriving at the Nyabingi, a hilltop site cleared from a forest of trees, at the foot of which flowed a small river under ferns and bamboo. In twos, fours, singles, families, Rastas were arriving. With sighs and smiles of relief at having reached the place of celebration and union, they were making temporary camp under trees, spreading out brightly coloured cloths, flags and hammocks around the tabernacle.

For the next three days and nights each soul would be concentrating on nothing more than singing holy songs, chanting holy verses, and reasoning Holy reasonings on the Father JAH and His Son, Christ, made real to us through the livity of His Imperial Majesty, Emperor Haile Selassie I.

A Nyabingi was a special, precious and rare event, a chance for Rastafari to come together in the peace of the virgin countryside and – for a few precious hours – to live as we hoped to live in our homeland Zion.

We brought tents, rolled up beds, pots and pans, food, changes of clothing, but most of all we brought our love of JAH Selassie I, the mystical revelation of Christ that had been given to us – the lowest and poorest people on earth, and who by our revelation, had become the highest, I-est.

A Nyabingi was also a fire, hot fire, that penetrated hearts and souls, sought out wolves in sheep's clothing, asked point questions, put wayward dreads on trial whether present or not.

Many Rastas were absent, fearing the anger or judgement of one or other of the many gray-locksed elders gathered around the ever-burning fire in the tabernacle – elder dreads who were convinced that they had only to utter the word FIRE, for flames to devour whatever person or object they directed the word at.

But a "Bingi" was also a time of pure joyous love, when the musical harmonies of voices raised in the Nyabingi songs, poured out over the ever-drumming heartbeat of the big bass. The songs were a mystery to outsiders, but well-known to Rasta, and with brethren on one side and sisters on the other of the circular thatched shelter we called tabernacle, the music was unceasing, day or night.

Joseph knew he would be questioned this night. He knew that all the gathering knew he was a 'star', the first Rasta superstar. He knew they pretended that he was no different, but he saw them eyeing him, examining his behaviour for one trace of pride, arrogance, or special-ness.

Joseph knew they would find no fault with him. Here, he was happiest, most at home. Here he was equal with equals, and the heights of his life was to be in this place and this company forever. He intended to remain the same Joseph he had always been, for he knew that to change would cause JAH to take the Blessing form him, the blessing that had only come because he was a part of this very life around him.

So he waited until he was called to the centre of the circle, waited while the Psalm was read:

> *"Blessed is the man who walketh not in the counsel of the ungodly, nor standeth in the way of sinners, nor sitteth in the seat of the scornful..."*

He joined in the chant of the Psalm from memory, as all the others did.

Then he waited for the questions. But the questions were not harsh. For Joseph was loved, loved for his Christ-like simplicity, his happiness, and for his upholding of pure Rasta ways. So he relaxed, and let the words flow like cool water.

"What do you tell journalists, Brother Joseph?"
The question came from one of the elders. Joseph laughed a small laugh, but not of disrespect, but delight.

"When they ask me about the music, and why me play that hop-hop rhythm like a lame man walking, I tell them: Listen to the beat, then listen to your heartbeat. After they do that, they start to respect the rhythm."

Joseph spoke loudly, for he knew that hundreds of people here were keenly listening to his words, weighing them. He was under examination, by the harshest judges in the world, and the wisest.

The faces of the Elders were lined with deep furrows, their dreadlocks were hanging weights, edged with gray. Some wore serious expressions, like the warrior kings they had been in a younger time. Others were soft and mellow. But all had staring, deep-looking lion eyes, looking deep into the soul of this man who to them was simply one of their youths, grown on their beach since age 12 through the years to 17, when his mother had thrown him out of the house for smoking too much ganja.

"Good answer." said Elder Purrie.

Joseph smiled. "Fada Purrie, I grow in front of you Bredrin, and you turn me from a boy to a man, from a fool into a wise. I go fishin' many times with each and every one of you bredrin, leave early morning and sometimes don't come back for days."

"I run from police with you down here, "Elder Purrie laughed, "and get me first guitar while I a-rest a you' gates. Onoo Bredrin teach me wrong from right. I sit down here many nights, listening to you reason 'bout Africa and how we can get back Zion."

"I hear onoo chant BLOOD and FIYA to consume those who keep us here in captivity away from Zion – us and our mothers and fathers and our children and daughters. I know that bitter gall comes in the mouth of each and every one of us, from time to time, but I&I have the promise in the Holy Word, and the promise is fulfilled in His Imperial Majesty Emperor Haile Selassie I, RASTAFARI, Our Returned Messiah, whose Kingdom is now come."

"And whether Babylon wants to admit it or not, good is going to triumph over evil, and I&I a-go get what we want. One day."

"In the meantime, the Father JAH give I&I ways to present I&I case to the world, and I music is the most powerful way the father has given I&I, so I pray that what I learnt from you Elders and from the Book, will make me do the right at all times."

Such a powerful speech broke the tension of judgement. The questions that came now, sought the answers merely for their entertainment, and each answer brought loud laughter, or comments of "Wise", "Tell them, Joseph", "Ride on, Fari".

"What you tell them about dreadlocks, Joseph?" "Bway, them have so much questions about mi locks. Some want to know if is spit I use, some ask why I put cow dung in my hair."

"But I tell them say dreadlocks is the mark of the free Black man, because since we didn't have comb or razor on the slave ship, I can see that we land here as slaves, our hair was locks, and them had to trim and shave we before they put we on the block to sell we. I tell them that the locks is how them could know a runaway slave, because after a few days on the run, our hair would locks. So I tell them that I locks my hair to show that I-man is a free man.

"Them no like fi hear that answer."

The group laughed.
"What about Selassie I?" a voice spoke. "What you say about the King?"

"I tell them Christ promised to return and Rastafari say Christ returned to us as His Imperial Majesty, Emperor Haile Selassie I. I tell them I don't care whether they want to think like I or not. But I tell them to remember that the Jews didn't want to accept the fact that Jesus WAS the Christ. It was only his followers down the centuries that proved that He was indeed the One we were told would come.

"You know, many of the journalists are Jewish – is them control the media in America – and when I lick them with that one, it lick them HOT."

Everyone laughed. The drum pounded, and the rhythm penetrated the reasoning. An elder put up a chant:

> *The Niah-man, dem red, dread*
> *Rastafari bring down Babylon,*
> *Lightening burn down Babylon.*

Several harmonies were fused on to the main melody – two bass levels, three treble, and a high soprano from a sister whose fine voice sang out from behind blind eyes.

The songs and chants followed one after another into the pure night, each verse swelling loudly and sweeter. The drums were licked, hot, hot, hot. Those standing swayed in the one-two rhythm (no hip movement or wiggling allowed in this holy temple), while two Nyabingi warriors using their rods like spears, danced around the fire, locks flying, repeating the war dances of antiquity remembered through the anchor or their navel strings.   **RASTAFARI!!!**

In the watching hours before dawn, some slept, some sang, some waited for the brew of thick chocolate tea, boiled with cinnamon leaves, and served with fried cornmeal dumplings.

As dawn lighted, one by one people made their way to the nearby river to wash, bathe, and then give thanks and Praise to JAH, the Father, for LIGHT and LIFE

The drum beat had not ceased its rhythm since it had started yesterday afternoon, though many different hands had stroked the skin of the bass drum, when breakfast of fried fish, green bananas and callaloo was served. A brother shared some sugar cane with us, we gave him a draw from our well-filled bag. Joseph always had a bag of good herb. He never carried it, to discourage beggars, but from it we filled cutchies and built spliffs.

As we sat in the sun on the river bank, wiggling our toes in the wet sand, Niah Simon walked over to us, accompanied by a white man who was obviously an American. He wore a knitted skull cap in red, gold and green, glasses on his round, shiny face. Around his neck was a small leather African bag, and a camera, and he wore sandals on his feet. He was plump, but big, and didn't look slow, somehow.

He stretched out his hand before I-a Simon could introduce, and said in a strong voice:

"Hi Joseph, I'm Sam Bergam. I've been trying to meet you for a week now."

"Why?" Joseph asked.

"I'm a writer. Doing a book on Rasta. I want to interview you."

Joseph thought about this for a moment, then said "What you know about Rasta?"

"Nothing," the man replied. "That's why I want to talk to you."

"But how them have man whe' no know nuttin' 'bout Rasta, a 'write book on Rasta, when so much Rasta bredda and sista whe' can write, a-sit down a-yard, a-wonder how dem baby a-go eat food today?"

He said this to us, but we all knew his question was for this American, who seemed to be so far from the consciousness we all shared.
We waited for his answer.

"Well, my editor felt that the kind of book our American readers want about Rasta is one written by someone who already knows. So they asked me. I have a Ph. D in Sociology, and my thesis was on the Peyote Indians, who fought for and won the right to use their sacred mushroom, which is otherwise classified as a dangerous drug and weed, like LSD."

He waited to see if any of us knew or understood what he was talking about, but there was something about him that I didn't feel comfortable about, and I could see Joseph and his brethren felt the same, because they were even more closed up than they usually were around strangers. But we didn't give him a clue, so he continued:

"I arrived in Jamaica last week, and apart from trying to find you, I've been going around meeting other Rastas and people who want to talk about Rasta."

"Such as who...?" Joseph spoke.

"Well, I've spoken to Professor Hudson Granger. He was really interesting." Sam smiled proudly.

"Cho!" Bongo Hilly exploded from the rear of our group. "What can he have to say about Rasta. Him no know what is Rasta."

But quick as a flash, Joseph corrected him.
"No, I-ya, him can say a LOT about Rasta, for he is the opposite of Rasta, and yet he praise Rasta."

"How opposite?" the American asked, too quickly. The man they spoke of, was a University intellectual noted for his scholarly books, as well as for his genius as a theatrical actor.

"Well, Joseph explained. "He is the best product of the English system at work in her colonies, a very Black man trained in the highest institutions to adopt the values and habits of their civilization, and yet he cannot reject Rasta; he has to praise it even though he cannot live it. THAT is the power of Rasta."

"Is he a homosexual, as people say?" Sam asked Joseph directly. Joseph leaned his head to one side.

"Wha' dis bwoy a-ask me, eh? If I knew the answer to that I would be a battyman, myself. Me no business if him a-battyman, or not. Don't they say the Royal family of England have a whole heap of them as servants to the Queen?" He looked at us.

"If is so him want to live the Christ-life JAH give him, is him business that, for the Father done tell us what is the reward of sodomy in Romans Chapter One, and that sodomy is a sin without repentance. Me can see say is battyman a-rule the world right now, even here in Jamdown, but me nah deal with wha' dem say about the man – me a-deal with wha' HIM say bout' Rasta. Me would only like know why everyone who come a-Jamaica come look for Rasta, go check him."

"Well, I'm also here checking you and this Nyabingi," Sam bowled that ball back.

"True," said Joseph, outing the small end of the spliff, rose to his feet and started walking back to the Nyabinghi temple.

"But I haven't finished my interview!"
Sam started up after Joseph.

"I never know you start it!" Joseph was serious. "Well you got more interview than many,"

And with those words, he stepped forward and we followed him, moving over to the other side of the river, crossing the stones made smooth by the water passing endlessly over the shining gray curves.

The Nyabingi had regained its strength, as voices made happy by food and warm tea, by water and sunshine, sang out clearly in the sweet-smelling morning carrying our angel choir to the gates of Zion, and to the ears of HIM who sits beside the Throne of Thrones, to whom the songs of Praise are continually sung by the fortunate souls who have received their blessing reward.

> "A wha' dem a-go wit' Rasta
> When the las'day comes......

* * * *

We didn't see Sam the journalist for about a month. Joseph had been cooling out at Bull Bay getting some new songs, and I saw a lot of him because that was the beach I went to whenever I wanted to get away from Wareika and smoke free in the cool of the sea breeze.

Just getting off the minibus at Eleven Miles, was enough to freshen I mind, and the walk over the black sand path through macca and Lignum Vitae trees, was like travelling into a new world millions of miles away, where everyone was God and everyone was good.

"Love, Sis!" "Hail up, daughter." "How the I?" were the greetings I received as I walked, from those I knew and those who didn't even know I name.

Goats – JAH knows what they found to eat among the sand and macca – were everywhere under every shade, silently going about their gentle business. The sky and the sea were the same colour.

I and I sister swam in shift dresses, not conventional swim suites, as we did not want to expose ourselves any more than we did when we were not at the beach, especially to the brothers and elders – that would be impolite.

By the time we had swum, with plenty of diving under water and happy noises, I-ah Fuzzy would have cooked the one pot of vegetables, rice-and-peas in coconut milk, from the bag of food we brought with us for him, and made lemonade by sending a youth up the road to buy a small block of ice.

One of the days I was there, so was Joseph who offered me a lift back to town. "I'm going up by 1C Oxford Road," he said. "What's that?" I asked. "Come, find out." he replied.

One Cee, as the place was called by everyone, was the central meeting place of the Rasta/reggae music scene in the 70's, the headquarters to which every musician and person connected with the music in it's new found fame, was directed.

It was an old wooden Kingston house of yester-years, slightly refurbished and turned into a series of shops selling things like irie clothes, leather bags and shoes, and a restaurant serving salads and sandwiches.

To the rear, dreadlocks Johnny Evans ran his promotion and booking agency, hiring and touring the best of the reggae singers and musicians, choosing from a wide selection of stars and would-be stars who hung out at his office daily. Musicians would pass through looking for other musicians to make up a session, to see and hear new music being rehearsed in the garage that served as a rehearsal room, or just hanging out and drinking ital juices and burning spliffs. If you wanted to find anyone in reggae music, you could just hang out there for a while; they would pass through sooner or later.

Evans was arranging a tour for Joseph, and while they discussed it, I sat and watched the whole scene, like a movie unfolding that I now knew so well through being around Joseph.

There was so much that looked unreal. I saw men who had grown dreadlocks in the hope of stardom, or for fashion, but who by their behaviour showed themselves to be wolves in sheep clothing.

I saw women wearing skirts and sandals, but not prepared to go the whole Rasta way and cover their chief beauty, their hair – not realizing that it's beauty is an object of lust for men... or maybe they did. I saw photographers, and writers, trying to get contacts for books and articles on this star or other, and dreads trying to look important so someone would take their pictures.

And I saw some beautiful people – singers and players of instruments, who sang and played music because it was the only life they had ever known – known it in poverty before the Reggae Revival, would be poor throughout the heights of Reggae's popularity, and are still poor today when Reggae is no longer an exclusively Jamaican treasure – despite the great talent and righteousness they had.

Some receive, others don't. JAH knows who and why.
But these people graced our lives with their souls and their light.
For them all, One Cee was home.

"I saw Joseph in Evans' office."

The voice disturbed my thinking. It was Sam, the American.
I didn't bother to speak, hoping he would take the hint, and
move on, but he didn't. He continued.

"Joseph says I can come up tonight and do that interview. Could
you be there? I'd like to talk to you too. As a friend of his."

I considered this. "Joseph would have to say so."

"Say what?" It was Joseph, on the other side of the car.

Sam repeated his suggestion.

"Sure, Sister Shanty, come spend the rest of the day by I gates
and help reason with him."

I called Joseph into the car. Sam realized I wanted to be private,
and moved off a little from the car.

"I don't like this brother, you know. Joseph. He's kind of funny,
like he is not what he says he is. Do you feel it?" I was
concerned.

"Yes I do, Sister Shanty. But instead of running from him, I am
going to run into him and find out what he is really dealing with.
Help me, nuh? As a woman you can check him in a direction I
cannot, so you help me find out what dis man a-deal with."

To tell you the truth, I was glad to be going up the house,
because I didn't have a lick of food at my gates. The little factory
work I was on out west, had laid me off, and the money I had
used to bring food out to the elders on the beach, was all I had.
What was it my mother sent me to school to 5th form, when
there were no jobs, especially not for one who lived on Wareika?

At Joseph's at least I would get a bellyful, not to mention some good vibes to soothe the frustration of life.

Up at the big old house, the new Cubs were rehearsing for the tour, and the noise of music, interrupted by corrections, and then played over again, dominated all activities. Joseph relaxed and played some football with some of the usual crowd of idren who were always there waiting for Joseph to kick a ball to them. As usual, Joseph was a one-man band that led and fed the entire team of his followers of all kinds.

Now Joseph had an organization to help him; a manager – a sharp Kingston con-man well suited for dealing with the shady people who made the tour and record contracts; a "special assistant" - Busha's cousin – a brown St. Andrew princess who locksed after being found with herb by Police at a Nyabingi camp.

There was a fat, ever happy dread - the roadie - who had been known to pack a speaker box with so much herb that he made more out of the tour than Joseph had been paid, bringing it in without a moment'sproblem just by swearing and shouting in broad Jamaican at the 60 pieces of equipment before two young American customs officers, who were simply terrified of this large Rastaman who looked like he could pick them up and fling them across the room just like he was flinging bits of equipment and luggage.

Not forgetting the Bag Man to carry the herb and build spliffs, who often was listed as 'cook' on the travel list. Joseph supported his entire team, and also sent money to Rosy to care for her two children – one his – as well as the baby mothers of his three other children.

Not to mention such as me – loving those warm times in the old house shaded by cool trees, and everyone full of the warmth of love; love expressed in friendly smiles and peaceful understanding built on the knowledge of the Father JAH and the effort to follow in the footsteps of the King of Peace.

Sam arrived at about seven and found us sitting under the ackee tree in the back yard, enjoying some good herb and digesting a good meal. He said he had already eaten, but accepted a glass of fresh cheery juice as he set up his tape recorder and adjusted his cameras.

"Sister Shanty, look upstairs you see a tape recorder. Bring it and let us take a copy of his interview." Joseph ordered me.

That's how I come to be a permanent part of Joseph's team, a kind of librarian and press contact in times to come. That's how I can re-play the interview for you now.

*　*　*　*

SAM: How does it feel to be the Leader of the Rastafarian movement?
JOSEPH: *Wha! Don't mek me laugh. Me a-no leader of Rasta. Me a jus' ordinary Rasta. Rasta no have no leader,. Every man is his own leader, because Selassie I set the example.*

SAM: What example?
JOSEPH: *The example of Christ in flesh. The King of Peace returned to gather his flock.*

SAM: Those are very controversial words, Joseph. A lot of people would disagree with you and say you are mad.
JOSEPH: (LAUGHS) *YES. But a lot of people see how possible it is, that statement is true, and some are full believers, while some are just watching and waiting. But I&I know that by now the world can see that the real Rasta is the real way Christ said we fi live.*

SAM: How is that?
JOSEPH: *OK, you are one of those. Well, if you want to hear, listen. When Jesus Christ left us, he promised to return, yes? Well, remember when He came the first time, the Jews said He was not the Messiah, because the Messiah would come as King..*

Now this time He come again like He promised, and this time He has come as King, but once again the people who say they know who God is, say that this is not Christ. While a group of people that nobody of society check for, these humble people say Selassie is Christ come again. And to prove it, a whole lot of people a-try live like Christ, because Selassie showed them the light.

So who is wrong? Who is foolish? The people who say they know Christ? The people who go to church every Sunday, or Saturday, or every night, do they live like Christ..?

The Pope who blessed Mussolini to invade Ethiopia, the Church of England who blessed the slave ships – all these churches, what have they done that is Christ-like towards the condition of the Black Man?

Those Churches never teach me anything except Bible Verses. They never teach my sisters say they mustn't kill their unborn babies in the womb. They never teach my brothers not to shoot a man for a bag of money.
Rasta teach those things today, so I check say Rasta must be God.

SAM: How did you become Rasta?
JOSEPH: *Bwoy – it is a thing born in you. You don't become a Rasta. You come to know Rasta in you.*

But if you mean, when did I know – I used to be a youth work on the brown man's plantation, before I run away to town. I used to go and hitch up outside a yard where they use to sell herb and chant Nyabingi – they called it a church, but it was just a yard. And I used to hear them sing the Nyabingi songs and, y'unnow – like any youth, I would sing them when I was in the field by myself.

Well one of them times busha catch me a – sing: "What you going to do with Rasta in the last day..." at the top of my voice, and called me and tell me say if I can't sing any better song than that beard-man song. I must find another job.

56

That was the first time I realize that the songs had a power to pierce the heart of the wicked, for Busha was a real old wicked, and I was glad to find that could jook him. So me start listen the songs more and then I go inside the yard a few times and listen the reasoning.

And, to how I study the beard man-them, and I listen to their word-sound, I decide that was the side I want to res' on. It was the first I ever hear 'bout Africa, and a time when Black man was great, and as a little yout', I was glad, y'un now.

SAM: But you're half white. Wasn't your father European? How can you look only to Africa for cultural roots?

JOSEPH: *Well first of all, the European side of me already been filled full of knowledge about Missus Queen and Henry Morgan and all that stuff from when me did a-go school. So me know bout dat already.*

But nobody tell I about Africa at all, except that we were naked slaves. And when you look at it, no matter how much white blood I have in me, I will always be considered Black by Black and White. So is not me to choose Black – the choice already mek for me by the world.

SAM: Why this preoccupation with race and colour? Aren't we all brothers?

JOSEPH: *A-no me concerned with colour. Black people is all colours, even white. Is you, the White man, that categorize us, and classify us, so that some of us can read and some can't; so that some can slave for you in one way, and some another.*

Is you make the division, and I suffer from it.
So my songs and my life are to heal the wound and show you and me what we must do to free ourselves and live together in a world of peace.

SAM: You believe that's possible? A world of peace?

JOSEPH: (laughs) *Of course. Don't you pray everyday: Thy Kingdom come on earth? Whose Kingdom? The King of Peace, of course! Heaven on Earth will come, and in our time too.*

SAM: So you see yourselves as a kind of John the Baptist come to prepare the way?

JOSEPH: *Is why this man trying to set me up, eeh? Is kill you want them kill I?*

Me not no John the Baptist; Me not nothing. Me a jus' Joseph Planter, and if you like I songs, you sing the tune. Is jus' the Father JAH sen' I here for.

Take a break now! Take a break. Now tell me something. Why is it I feel like you are a police, cross examining me? That's what I don't like about this "interview". You mek me feel like you a CIA.

You can hear our voices agreeing with Joseph, with serious sounds. Someone, I forget who, started cleaning his nails with his ratchet knife. Sam looked around at us, at the door, and then to the verandah – all out of his reach, then spoke.

"I knew you would say that, when I asked the questions I knew I was going to ask." he answered.

"Those are not the questions you are use to; usually you are interviewed by fools seeking knowledge. I am a wise one, seeking information. If you are wise, you can use me to give information. If you are wise, you can use me to give whatever information you want to the world, just as you want it said, and I will give it."

"Why should I? For what gain?" Joseph asked.

Sam laughed. "First, because I know I can make a lot of money doing it. I have access to the biggest and best publishing houses, who are waiting eagerly to get a genuine book on you and your movement, because the American public is very curious."

He paused before continuing. "Second... because, like you, I also want to be on the winning side and you – and what you stand for – could be the Truth."

There was a deep meditative silence all around, when he said this. A thousand questions raced through our heads, we looked at Joseph, at each other. Without asking permission, I spoke:

"Why should you be the one to make money from our words and lives and religions? It should be us, who should reap – someone of our race."

Sam smiled, leaned back in his chair, and put his arms behind his head.

"You're absolutely right, Sister Shanty. But, you see, the white world feels the same way about themselves, so they say if they are going to create a money-making vehicle, then their own people must make money all along the way."

I growled at his answer, but he just laughed again.

"Oh! I'm sure some of your good writers and creative people will come up with some good works, but you'll find publishers hard to co-operate, and then you'll try publishing it yourselves, and find out how hard distribution is and how closed-up the business is, and you'll end up poorer, bitter, and frustrated at your efforts. Yes, I'm white, but I am your door to the world and especially to the rich world. Take it, or leave it."

"How do we know we can trust you to tell the whole world the truth as we see it and speak it?" Joseph asked.

"You have only my word," he replied. "Other than that, you have no guarantee that I, or anyone else, won't exploit and misquote or misuse the work I do here tonight, or any other occasion. You just have to trust your God. JAH? Yes?"

There was another deep silence, while we considered this, also.

Then Wooly said: "Mek the man g'wan, yah. What him write can't kill I&I – all is from the Father JAH, Alpha I, Selassie I. Let him write, for is him the Father has sent."

Joseph leaned his head on one side, as he used to, resting his chin on his fingers, considering. Then he straightened up, looked Sam full in the eyes, and said:

"You pass a test, so you can continue. But this will not be the last test. Remember that."

The two looked at each other, locked in mental bands, as tough as warriors in combat.

Finally Sam said: "I'll remember that."

"You haven't asked me about the herb yet," Joseph said with a laugh that broke the tension. "Build a spliff for the white man, Wooly, and one for I."

With that, the interview continued in a better vibe, more free, more understanding, more giving,... we were more comfortable to be with this man, even to allow photos to be taken. This was the first of many such talks Joseph had with Sam, the American. If this was a movie, you would now have a scene with printing presses rolling off copies of books of all kinds, because Sam was to use these talks as the basis for many books and articles he wrote about Joseph over the years and after his death – books full of good clear photos and articles; books that took the messages of Reggae to all corners of the world; books that translated Rasta into the English of the non-ghetto world, Black and white; books that made Sam rich.

The last time he and I spoke, Sam was boasting of how easy it was for him to write a book now, on his new word processor. I am writing this book by hand with pen and pencil, can't help feeling some envy and anger still that he has got so much from just being the one privileged to reach so close to Joseph.

He did ask an interesting question though. He asked Joseph how it was that he did not obey Rasta rule that woman was inferior and unclean, but instead had many women and allowed them into his inner circle.

Joseph threw back his head and laughed, long
"That a-no Rasta rule – that is rascal rule. Me LOVE woman.
And so I should, for woman is I, and I am woman."

SAM: How do you reason that?

JOSEPH: *Well, the Father is Creator and He made mankind in His image. Well, for Him to create man and woman, he has to be Man and Woman too. For example, when He was to make Christ, He went with a woman, Mary. So to make Adam, He was both Man and Woman. And Woman is also His image, like He says. Woman is the other half of me that makes a complete copy of God – JAH. So woman couldn't be inferior, she had to be equal, else she and I could not unite in equality and produce a child like JAH.*

SAM: So when you are with a woman you are God?

JOSEPH: *Well... I guess you could say that, but only if she is seen as God also, for I couldn't be with an inferior.*

SAM: Why do you smoke ganja?

JOSEPH: (sighed, took a deep draw and answered.)
In the madness of people lost from sight of their God, unable to see the beauty of the wind or feel the power of a bird's morning song, the herb is my golden cord to heaven, bringing me to the peace, love and sanity that prevails in Zion.

Zion, choice and happy place, where my minds of His divine intellects converse all day and night in silent meditation, singing hymns of Praise to JAH, the Father, and Christ, His Son.

Yes, man, the herb allow I to recall such heights and stay there for my benefit to enable I to live and survive down here in Babylon.

And because the herb puts I in touch with I Father JAH, Satan and his angels fight I down.

Yu'know, Jamaica would be heaven if everyone was allowed to smoke herb.

But politicians rule. For who is fighting down the herb? No politicians? So who is the enemy and why? The answer, is power to rule. Either JAH rule or politicians rule.

But is a battle they goin' lose. Mus' have to lose.

So since I&I know that, they can't kill I&I for herb, I jus' gwine gwaan smoke it and tek' remembrance of I Father's Kingdom, and the mansion He is preparing for I.

* * * *

It was about one in the morning, that Sam ran out of questions, and Joseph got tired of speaking. We prowled the yard, listened to some late-night music on the radio, then Joseph told Sam to give me a lift home, sending Small Youth to accompany him back, and to chaperone me through the night streets.

It was strange for me, driving in front with a white man, making myself small in the small car's seat, in case his hand changing gear might touch me, speaking only to give him directions, yet very conscious of him looking at – into – me, as often as he could.

Finally we reached my gate, and he jumped out of the car, leaving the engine running, and came around to open the door, which I had already opened, but he tried to help me out and walked behind, and opened the gate of the house, and when I turned to say Thanks, he told me he wanted to come check me some time to reason about Rasta Woman.

"Like, I want to know why you Rasta women always cover up yourselves, like you are ashamed of your beauty," he said. "You are beautiful; you should let it show."

I sighed.

JOSEPH - A RASTA REGGAE FABLE

"That is the philosophy of the women of Babylon," I answered him. "I am not ashamed of my beauty. I know how beautiful it is, how it can rise up the sap in a man, just by a glimpse of the soft smooth skin of my upper legs, or my arms, or even the mysteries of my hair. The men of Babylon like to spend their time contemplating such visions, and the women of Babylon keep their men forever weak by filling their minds with lustful thoughts.

"I, as Rasta woman, prefer to keep I&I lions on Zion filled with spiritual thoughts, so that they can be strong, and win our battles. We reserve the beauty of our bodies and our crowning glory, for the sight of our King Man alone.

"Now that is all the reasoning you will ever get from me, as a Rasta woman. A man shouldn't reason with a sister unless she is his woman, or he wants her to be. Since I am neither, find someone else to reason with."

I pushed the gate open, and stepped through.

After that night, I always kept my distance from him. I really didn't like him at all, and the more money he made from Rasta, the more I disliked him over the years. Yet, he stuck like a macca that you couldn't get out of your skin, and he grew to be as much a part of Joseph's circle, as I was to be.

CHAPTER FOUR

"Sing unto GOD(JAH) praises to his name: extol HIM that rideth upon the heavens by his name JAH, and rejoice before HIM." PSALM 68, V.4

We spent some good times together, those early days, days of waking up late after a night on the beach, reasoning with Rasta elders, waking up to peanut milk blended by Dusta and seasoned callaloo and fat boiled dumplings.

The parade of friends and others through the old house would begin. First the herbsmen, bringing the good calli; the the beggars, forever seeking a free spliff ... 'a money'; then the admirers would start coming around ten o'clock, perhaps a journalist or photographer from abroad. These included a lot of girls and women passing as journalists, just to get close to Joseph.

Some of them he would run them away, by being as cold as he and his brethren knew well how to be. We women friends would take the signal, and shun the women too.

But often he was flattered by the smiling interest some woman of beauty took in him, until it became a game for him and his brethren to study her and question her until her true motives, and hopefully, spirituality, were exposed rather than lust. At those times when a woman was truly able to hold his mind either by her silence or by her words, a deep sigh would come over Joseph, and he would rest on the love offered, almost like a man taking bitter medicine, mixed with honey.

Rest is the right word. Tropic owned many good resting places, where select people could be alone in the beauty of nature, and the very best comforts. So, now and then a woman took his fancy, and if Zuelika was abroad working, he would enjoy his fancy. By midday, we would begin an informal tour of the downtown studios, seeing who was hanging out there, or hearing new sounds.

Food would be had at one of hundred stopping places offering Ital food, juices, coconut water, sugar cane, and the afternoon would be lazily spent.

By dusk, the crowd at the old house had dwindled, some chased out by rudeness from Joseph or his posse to those he didn't want around; others had gone forth to other irie yards to hang out, reason smoke.

Evening would see the real idren arriving – the man-dem who only travel by night, who would sit in shadows under the trees in the yard and bring out some GOOD herb, and Joseph would bring out some GOOD songs, or some GOOD reasoning, and we would all give thanks to JAH for giving us such a WONDERFUL DAY.

*   *   *   *

It was 1976, and the politics was hot, well hot. Every day and night shots buss'ing all over the ghetto. Some of them uptown too. Uptown man getting as 'fraid as downtown man.

What they shooting for, I don't know. Gunshot never mark ballot papers, don't them foolish youths know that? They can only frighten people for a while, but sometimes gunshots lose election faster than it win.

Man know that, but you think they would gwan like they know it? No sah. So gunshots raining all over town. Everybody hiding inside at night, and sometimes daytime too.

Screech!
Brakes drew up beside me.
It was Skanker, a youth from Windward Road, on his big Honda bike.

"You know the boy they call Robert?"

"Yes," I said.

"Them shoot him this morning. Him, and some politicals out-a seaside."

His voice was frantic. Sweat ran down from his cap over his forehead. He looked over his shoulder anxiously, before he spoke next.

"Is a plot to kill off all the rebels. Peter sen' me to get you."

Peter is my King-man. I first met him at GP (the General Penitentiary) 1974 at the Prisoners Concert they were holding for the first time ever, first time ever prisoners got the chance to mingle with outsiders, especially women. First time ever they got a chance to mingle some revolutionary prison poems among the bittersweet hymns and schooldays recitations that composed this concert of forgotten souls.

Two thousand forgotten souls, four thousand eyes looking piercingly into eyes and hearts of the two women who had been brave enough to venture behind the walls of solitude and brutality.

It was Peter who had stood up, eased himself out of the crowd and taken centre stage to recite Maya Angelou's poem:

> *"I know why the cage bird sings....*
> *The cage bird sings, because the memory of freedom is sweet."*

I could not help looking back into those searching eyes, I could not help looking into the openly-presented heart of this man who, if he even had been guilty of a crime, showed in his entire bearing his strength of voice and person, that he had long been cured of whatever error and whatever sadness had brought him to this ugly, barren place.

How he had gotten my address afterwards, I don't know. It's apart of the prison grapevine, knowing how to contact people. Anyway, he started writing to me, letters in which he poured out his passions – passions which were revolutionary, not sexual.

Which made him unusual, interesting and exciting.
He wrote me a letter, and I replied in general terms. His second letter was more revealing:

> *"Black blessings, Sister Ashanti,*
> *It was a most enlightened moment to have met you. The simplicity and human relationship which you expressed amongst us, the Rebel Slaves of an unjust society, clearly showed that there are Black Women who are truly aware of the plight of Black Man from the slums. Such communal relationships are the fundamental elements which aid in the building of a classless society, wherein all are interlinked as one Big Happy Family.*
>
> *"Experience has shown me that no totally oppressive, suppressive and unjust society, which has a built-in strategy within it's political system geared to divide and rule. Enclosed is a poem. Let me hear your critics on it, if you wish.*

> Black Beauty! Black Pearl!
> Who are you?
> We have searched for
> Thy African-ness so long.
> Open the windows of thy soul,
> And let your People Shout!
>
> Black Mother, Black Majesty!
> Thy warriors are thy protectors.
> Your enemy our footstool.
> Come! O Black Woman
> And let thy African-ness be seen
> Come, O Woman of Fertility
> Thy guidance we need."

I didn't know what kind of answer to send to this letter, and I took a while thinking about it. Obviously. I took too long, for he soon wrote me again.

"Dear Sister.
Why, having taken the initiative to pay me compliment
of writing to me amidst this aura of frustration and
brutality, have you chosen to deny me the continuation
of this pleasurable relationship? Have you in a moment
of retrospection, regretted having even briefly cast a
glimmer of light in this my world of darkness and pain?
If so, then according to the underlining principles of
freedom of thought and action I, must accept your
decision. Though my whole being is twisted in agony,
my mind unsettled.

You see, Ashanti, my greatest and most potent wish is to
see, and ardently work for, our relationship to grow
and bloom into firm, purifying Oneness. As you are
aware, such an accomplishment can in no way be
attained without mutual give and take within a positive
aura." PETER

I smiled when I read this, and realized how important my letters
to him were. So I started a regular correspondence.

His sentence had ten months left to run, when without warning
the authorities increased another five months... said he had
been one of the leaders of a hunger strike against prison
conditions. But Peter wrote to me that he had no more to do
with the hunger strike, than sharing with other prisoners his
legal copy of Huey Newton's book "Seize the Time"...

Oh Peter, my sweet Peter.... Five years for a crime he never did,
served it all, having to do five months more.

Never mind, I wrote to him. Time will soon pass. It will soon be
over. The anger of his reply was unexpected:

"Ashanti:
Do you truly believe that there is no real difference
between April and August? No difference in spending
four more months, 120 more days, under this
maddening, sadistic process, a process specifically

68

JOSEPH - A RASTA REGGAE FABLE

geared – regardless of the pretty oratory made by both past and present regimes – to either mad the individuals within their grasp, and/or aid in breaking up the family unit, build up the criminality and make one chronically dependent on the system and the handouts of the hidden hands behind the system? No. I really do not accept the thought that you truly believe this, that you would have given your blessings to the continuation of this heinous, sinister, brutal torturing wrapped up in its various window dressings.

"I think that you, Sis, being unaware of the grim reality that is the backlash of the present penal system, did not fully grasp the negative consequences of four full months or even four weeks within these slave camps. Please, Ashanti, never in the wildest moment of irrationality condemn your worst enemy to the treatment meted out behind these walls. It's gruesome.
At least you are comforting enough to advise me to have Faith. Indeed, Faith at its best enlivens the whole being of your body and spirit. At its worst, we live in a valley of despair and constant doubts. Without this most vibrant catalyst, which tears down and dismantles the castle of doubt within us, we are like 'the straw that goeth before the wind', pawns in the game of the powers-that-be.

"Faith is a necessary element in an intimate relationship, a positively unifying force. It ignites the ones consciousness an awareness of trust, and becomes a cleansing power. Faith, walking hand in hand with wisdom, leads one to the oasis of happiness, opening up the deep recesses of the Self, the God within us.

"Please, I beg you, pray as hard as you can that nothing further happens to keep me away from the freedom of the sky and the breeze and the light of sun on flowers.
Pray as hard as you can, that nothing happens to keep me waiting much longer for the precious pleasure I plan to have of holding you in my arms and resting in your

warm embrace, – even if that embrace is brief and promises nothing more than itself. I can cope with that briefness, so long as there is hope of its happening. That is what I live for each day, counting each day until that blessed event occurs.
Pray, Jah Sister, pray."

And pray I did. No words of a man had ever moved me like the words in those letters from prison, from Peter.

That was two years ago, and from that moment of our embrace (at the home of my friend Sharon which was his first stopping point on the day of his release), we had been together.

The house I shared with my sister was not too small to hold another soul, and on the nights when he stayed with me, it was heaven to lie beside him in the small bed, listening to the sounds of the night insects, listening to him telling of the experiences of prison, the horrors, the pain, the brutalities, of listening, until he was unburdened, washed free, almost whole again.

The pain subsided, but the memories never left him, nor his anger. This he channeled into grass roots political activity in the Wareika community – lecturing to the youths to avoid crime and badness, guiding the young warriors in strategic evasions of Babylon, teaching the baby mothers and fathers how to show love to their children in the midst of suffering, hunger and deprivation. In those two years, Peter had become a respected and loved leader of our community.

*   *   *   *

Skanker's bike roared up the rugged hillside roads, through tracks in the macca trees, behind one-room wooden houses, scattering mangy dogs and children, raising up clouds of dust, until finally we came to rest in the middle of what looked like a forest of trees, where a hut made of tree limbs and coconut thatch was Peter's hiding place.

Peter's first concern was where we could run to.

"We've got to get out of town. Too many people know me here, and how to find me. Too many youths being beaten for information."

Where could we go? We thought for a while.

Maybe we should go up to Joseph and see what he suggests, I said. He could easily hide us in the big house where only trusted friends could penetrate the private rooms. Peter agreed. We waited till dark, and then made a swift move on Peter's bike carrying only what could be packed into a big backpack.

Joseph and Peter had never met before. When I have a man, I like to keep him private for as long as possible. Especially since Peter was an old GP man, the need for privacy seemed greater.

I climbed off the bike and made my way up to Joseph's private quarters. He was resting on the verandah which was almost completely hidden by the branches of an old guango tree. I and I King-man need your help, I told him.

"Bring him come, mek me meet him," Joseph said.

They surveyed each other like lions at first, neither speaking. But then Joseph seemed to sense the tension in Peter and he could see how anxious I was, so he relaxed and said: "Come inside, me idren. You pick a good wife: I should-a pick her myself." And we all laughed and the tension disappeared.

Joseph gave up his upstairs apartment for us, and we made ourselves comfortable. There was a hammock slung across the verandah, and cushions on the wood floor; fruits, peanuts and water on a table beside us. We realized this was the first meal of the day for us, and soon there was only an empty plate.

Joseph, still testing Peter, looked at his short still growing locks, and asked whether the locks were a sign of Faith or just simply a mark of badness.

"Well Peter is Fari," I said, "but he is the kind of Rasta who believes that 'the System' won't change unless we ourselves take steps to liberate ourselves."

Joseph, as you know, believed that Faith, Prayer and Righteousness were the weapons that would make change, but I could see that he was interested in reasoning with a man who held such different views from himself.

One thing they were agreed on, though. The police action to 'clean up the ghetto' was merely a cover to eradicate the rebel youths who were becoming a threat to the political status quo.

"The rebel youths of an unjust society," is how Peter described them.

"We are hotting up the System, and the Big-Man-them don't like it. So they flood media with the story that we are ghetto gunmen, armed and dangerous, and that they have to kill us out before we kill innocent people. But in truth, is just that they 'fraid of how we reaching the people's minds, getting into their headspace, showing them that there is an alternative to this life of misery.

"Is the same thing you doing with your music, Joseph," Peter pointed out. " If they come for me tonight, tomorrow is for YOU, Joseph."

Joseph nodded, and drew on his spliff, thinking. We sat listening to his silence, waiting, fearing his response, hoping. Then he sat up in his hammock and spoke.

"You want we go St. Ann?"

Up we went at daybreak, up into the cool, bright St. Ann hills, to the dark red earth and emerald green pimento trees, to the little village where Joseph had grown up. There, on a small hillside overlooking the village, Joseph had built a wooden house, and it was there we stayed.

It was the most special time I have ever enjoyed with Joseph – and with Peter, though I hardly got a chance to speak with either of them, they were so tight with each other. As woman, I had the job of cooking and organizing, and you know how it is when there is only a wood fire you have to make each morning and keep alight during the day until the dumplings are fried, the coconut grated and squeezed into milk and poured into the pot of peas and vegetables and rice, until the callaloo is chopped ready to steam as soon as the rice and peas comes off the fire, and then the serving, and the walk to the spring to wash up everything and take a fresh.

By that time it is evening and the men are well rested and ready for the really important reasoning that seems to only come with night... you know how it is. But still even with all the work, it was really a pleasant activity for me, serving and taking care of two such special men, who in turn were taking care of me.

There we talked about Jamaica and politics and how to make JAH Kingdom come.

Joseph was curious. "How can you lick down the system by armed struggle? The man-them have so much guns and so much authority. Them can even call America and England to send soldiers to shot us down if we were to rise up our heads."

"How can you lick down this System unless you shot all them man them that is keeping it up. All the politicians, all the civil servants, the head of the radio station, even the Governor General. You have to kill them off, man, cut off their power over the people." That was Peter.

"Well," said Joseph, "The Father show I say I mus kill them off with music and with love, and with Truth. Tell them the truth, and in a loving way, in righteousness. Tell people to put love in their hearts, to right the wrong they did to the Black man in slavery and send us back home to our Motherland, Africa."

"What's the point of fighting for this rock," Joseph spread his arms, "when even while you are fighting, the white man is scooping out all the dirt and leaving us only the rock. Give me Ethiopia. Africa. Don't swop my Continent for an island that is just the modern version of the slave plantation it always has been."

"Cho." Peter was exasperated. "Your kind of Rastaman jus' caan' understand what we political Rastaman know – that only when we have power in our hands, can we use Jamaica as a ship to get us home. It's no use dreaming that JAH will come again, unless we become His army. We have to fight. That's the kind of warrior I am."

Joseph let Peter have the last word that night.

*   *   *   *

After we had been there for six days, we got a message that a secret meeting of ranking gang leaders was being held. We knew of the danger, but Peter decided to chance it, and flew across the island on his bike to the Wareika Gardens venue to hear what was happening.

Three days of my fretting later, he returned and by then we had heard on the radio about the Gang Truce in the ghetto, and how brothers and sisters who lived across the same street who couldn't cross it before the Peace, could now see each other and meet and greet, and how the Peace Pipe was being smoked day and night and music playing and everyone happy....they said.

"It is nice, really nice," Peter said when he told us about it. "But how long can it last?"

Peter also returned with an interesting proposal for Joseph: a benefit concert to seal the Peace, and they wanted Joseph to headline it.

Surprised, Joseph thought about it and discussed it with us. He didn't want to do it, to get involved, to show any allegiance with the political side of the ghetto and Rasta. But Peter used Joseph's own arguments to persuade him.

"This concert will end the war and seal the Peace. It's a way to win the Revolution with music. The war is over, but some man don't want to lay down their guns in case people say them coward. If you – the man they most admire in the world – come on stage and tell them to cool it with love, it will be okay."

And, to seal it, he said "They will be able to say: Is Joseph say me mus' cool."
Joseph saw the truth of this, even though his humility made him ask:

"Dem man dey will really listen to I?" Den, if me so powerful, is I should be leading the revolution!" And he stuck out his rooster chest and laughed, big, big.

"You are, JAH son." Peter looked him strong in the eyes.

Joseph got serious. "Don't repeat what I just said, ever, not even in a joke, you hear?"

He made us promise.

*   *   *   *

"You and Joseph ever made love?" Peter asked me bluntly, one night as we lay in St. Ann.

I smiled. "No. He did check for me once, but that was long ago in my father's yard, and since then we have become as brother and sister."

"Then you don't desire him, like all the other women?" he persisted.

I laughed.
"No. That is why Joseph likes me, likes having me around. He says it is nice to hear a woman's laughter. I don't interfere with his life, I don't judge, I don't chat too much. When the group travels, I do the things a woman can do – make telephone calls, shop for food in strange cities, we get along as a family."

"Okay." Peter seemed satisfied, and turned back to sleep.

"Hey." I nudged him. He turned back to face me.

"Don't ask me again, Okay? Put that thought away forever."
"It's done." he said, and embraced me warmly, one arm around my shoulders and one strong arm around my welcoming body.

*   *   *   *

It's hard to forget the weeks and days before the concert. An army of people, first from Tropic's New York PR Department, then from the Government's entertainment office, not forgetting all the ghetto war-lords and their bodyguards, took set on the old house, and by the time we came from St. Ann, the army was a well-drilled machine, each occupying a section of the house like a command post.

The air of excitement brought about by the presence of so many herbsmen and gunmen (and everyone pretending not to see them) was something marvelous to behold, for a one like myself who had little to do but watch, and sometimes cook food. We felt certain the police would raid the place, but then we felt certain they could not.

The fashion dreads, with their designer red-gold-green clothes, were also there, making sure they would be given tickets to the backstage area on the night where all the trendies would meet and greet.

The technical crew were in serious discussions, mostly to make sure their cash was paid up front – no 'for charity' for them. And in the middle of it all, the leaders of the Truce planning the speeches they would make on the night, changing them minutely and creating more and more dramatic things to say.

Peter and I were once again on the verandah, and Joseph often came up here to escape the crowd, and the journalists. But he wasn't happy; it was like he was patiently waiting, like a caged cat, anxious, before this, of all shows. One of the times he came up, I asked him what was wrong.

Joseph stopped walking up and down, and flung himself unto a pile of pillows.

"I don't know. That's just what I want to know. What's wrong. Something is wrong, and I can't see it, but I feel it. Is like the dreams I used to have when I first met Rosy."

He almost never spoke of his wife Rosy, a girl-woman who was the first ever to make him feel that his pointed nose and red colour skin were not something to be laughed at. Rosy reminded Joseph of his mother, raped by the white man in whose St. Ann house she worked. Rosy cured him of the terrible nightmares he used to have as a teenager, after he ran away from St. Ann to seek a life as a ghetto youth, hustling his day's bread. Dreams of violence, fights, pain.

He told us of the dreams, dreams that didn't explain themselves until life followed the dream and became reality. He had such a dream before he punched down the man who spat at him and called him a dirty Rasta on a New York street. If the incident had happened in the white part of town, you would have read of it in the papers; but since it was in Harlem, it was just another ghetto battle, soon over.

But blood was shed then.
And there had been other times.
"Guns will be there," Joseph said. "Every man going to bring his gun."

Peter sat up from the hammock. "Oh no. That's one part I insisted on. No guns. Every man will be searched by me and MY posse. A man at each gate."

Joseph digested this. Then he eased the worried from slowly off his face and lay back on his arms.

"Got to just wait."

CHAPTER FIVE

"And one of the elders saith unto me, Weep not: behold the Lion of the Tribe of Judah, the Root of David, hath prevailed to open the book, and to loose the seven seals thereof.
REVELATION 5: V5

There was a full moon the night of the show, and the Stadium was packed and full of excitement. Everyone was smoking a spliff, it seemed except the straight uptown people, who came to see.

We came down before Joseph, and spent some time backstage, saying hello and seeing who was there, while the early acts arrived. Peter came and went, checking on his stations and men. Then, finally he signalled me, and we moved out into the crowd, just as Robert Hands was starting his set, a speech set to music and he hit out against the way of life which had forced youths to become tribal warriors. He called for the legalization of herb, and took out a large spliff, so big the crowd roared out loud to see it – and lit it, calling on the Commissioner of Police to come arrest him.

Then surprisingly, he called on the Government to make Ethiopian Orthodox Church the national church of Jamaica. This was met some shouts of joy, as well as hoots of 'No Way' from those loyal to another mansion of Rastafari, for all mansions were here tonight.

When Robert sang his final song, the powerful *"Rise Ethiopians, We Mek Jah Yah"*, the crowd was like the roar of a lion.

Into the spotlight stepped Joseph, and we were at once aware that he didn't intend to try and outdo Robert and bring the crowd higher.

No way; he was going to cool out the vibe. And he stretched out that hand like he always did, and pointed it to the moon fully risen now over the crest of Wareika, and said:

"JAH"
"RASTAFARI" yelled every throat, 20,000 lions roaring.

"JAH" he said again.
"RASTAFARI" they roared again.

"JAH" he said, a third time.

And over their roar of "RASTAFARI", he hit his guitar one lick.
The drums went Bup, bap.
And the bass went Bu-dup-dup
and he hit the first notes of
"Behold How Good and How Pleasant."

As the old Rasta chant poured out like a flute from the Mighty King's mouth, the vast field was quiet, everyone still, straining to use their ears as a cup to keep the sweet water of the song and the singing in their minds forever.

By the time he reached the first chorus, "Brethren, dwell together in I-nity", some voices far in the bleachers had picked up the harmony, and by a few more lines, you realized that people in the stands had brought drums and were keeping the rhythms; while on the field dreadlocks were dancing with respectful faces and eyes lifted up to Heaven.

JAH! It was like angels swarming, I can't say it any other way. Like a lot of angels gathering together, more and more, as people put voice or drum or hands to increase the power of the song.

The song was US. Joseph had united us all, just with a simple song.

We waited, holding the last note, to see what he would do. He held the silence for one moment. He looked out over the vast crowd, slowly moving his eyes, like he could look into every eye.

Then he held the mic and said:
"Remember this moment."

With a snap of his finger, he broke the spell, hopping with a big grin, into a medley of his best hits, killing us with his jokes, happy laughter, feeling good feelings of irieness. People looked at perfect strangers and smiled. The foreign press was busy snapping photos of it all, and the jet set superstar who everyone was pretending not to see, looked around at this crowd of people who were paying him no notice, as they stood hypnotized by this simply dressed Rastaman on a small stage out there.

Just as we had begun to think that this was going to be just another show, Joseph signalled the band to an abrupt stop, and with a complete change of attitude, started to speak.

"Well, LOVE, mi bredrin and sistren. RASTA LOVE!
You all know why were here tonight.
To make Peace.
To make Love."

There were a few sniggers from the audience.

"No, not love like that. Love, like how JAH love we, like how Christ gave His life for us, and like how He rose again as Selassie I so that I and I could learn of JAH and find his salvation. THAT kind of Love me a-talk 'bout."

The crowd rustled, but was silent.

"Plenty of the other kind of love around, or so they say. That is how plenty of you and I come to be standing here tonight.... that kind of Love bring us here. But tonight me dealing with real Love, JAH Love, love between all of us. You. Me. Herbsman, locksman, politician, dread and baldhead."

The crowd was still now, giving Joseph full attention.

"JAH Love, me a deal with. So I gonna give you some Love songs. Because without Love, this ghetto Peace will be nothing more than a political stunt, and we don't need anymore of those – enough of we dead already."

And with that, he turned his back to the audience, to give the band the lead into his song *"Love All"*.

It was one clear shot, and it stained his back red, through his denim jacket.

*   *   *   *

Everyone was running everywhere; there were women's screams, men's shouts, noises of people falling, crying out as knives tried to slash way through the crowded panic.

Gunshots clappered the night, even some machine gun fire, police maybe, but more likely rebels. There was frenzy, as people clawed at clothes, hair, bodies, in a rush to escape.

"Stand still! Don't move!" It was Peter's command, and I had obeyed out of instinct, though my heart was pounding so hard it was like a bass guitar, and my adrenalin was trying to move my legs and body in the same mad rush as others.

His advice was correct. Falling and fallen chairs soon made us an untouchable island, around which people rushed, avoiding us. Soon the area around us was bare of people, so that we were conspicuous standing up.

"Lie down," he ordered, "On the ground."
The flattened and overturned chairs were a perfect cover for us, a barricade for Peter.

The lights around the Stadium were going out. Others in similar trapped or barricaded positions were seeking the cover of darkness. Peter aimed his gun at the stage lights, then at the main fuse box, which exploded in a shower of sparks and smoke as the bullets hit it.

We lay still, listening to the silence of waiting warriors, and now and then the cries of pain, and occasional gunshots. Then, soon, it was all dark – even the moon had disappeared.

"Quick" said Peter. "Gate 7 is ours. We control."

We jumped the barricades and started running. We ran, stumbled, fell, got up, ran again, until my breath was a hoarse rasp in my throat, and my heart a pumping motor.
An ambulance waited outside.

"A who dat?"
"Man...you wan' dead?"
"Is me... Peter."
"Seen. Safe."

And then on foot across Mountain View Avenue, and up the Long Mountain Trail to Wareika Hills, through the macca trees and scrub bushes on the dark side of the mountain, to the plateau on the top – two hours of run and walk, but then
..... at last ......
..... on the top ......
..... the very top .....
..... and safe.

We lay down the dew grass, and rested, drinking in air like water.

Two days we hid there, Peter and I and some others who knew of this hiding place, sharing peanuts from the sack of a brother who had hidden his gun in his vending basket, and drinking water from bamboo roots.

I can't tell you who sent the helicopter for us, the one with false JDF colours, but we were really GLAD to see it. We ran under the blades and were grabbed up into it as it swooped up Peter and me and one dread who wouldn't let go. Then we swung across the harbour over the Palisadoes to Lime Cay, where we were lowered onto a big yacht, bound for one of the Bahama islands first, then on to Miami – a ganja boat.

We were in Miami for two weeks.

*   *   *   *

"They've killed him," she sobbed repeatedly, over and over, banging her fists on the soft, overstuffed brown velvet cushions of the James' living room sofa.

Evelyn James drew hard on her cigarette in its black ebony holder, and sighed.

"Darling, stop being so dramatic, or you'll have us believing you love him or something."

"But I do!" Zuelika looked up with a wet face. "How can you be so cruel? You're my best friend!"

Evelyn crossed her leg angrily. "Maybe that's why I'm trying to get you to be realistic."

The James' were very wealthy, English, and had known Zuelika since the first days she had come to England. John James had literally picked her up at a bus stop in Knightsbridge and brought her home to Evelyn as yet another curiosity of their privileged life. The James' fortune had been made from 17th Century Jamaican sugar and they had always had a Jamaican or two among their dinner guests. Zuelika's growing fame had made her a fixture in their lives for longer than most, and she and Evelyn often went shopping together.

When Busha became Zuelika's man, the James happily welcomed him into their circle. Evelyn fancied herself a singer, and when the entertaining in the chocolate brown living room, would often open up the piano and play musical games with her guests, reserving for herself solo pieces where she could display her voice. The thought that her songs were much older than her guests, did not matter to her, though aging did, and Zuelika made her forget her age and her gray hairs.

For Zuelika, the James' were the parents she wished she had always had and with whom she could be the person she was now, not the person she had been. With her good looks, her admirers and happy laughter, Zuelika gave the James' access to her showbiz world, in return for her access to their society.

And yet, here she was worrying because some ragged ghetto youths had shot and killed a semi-literate dreadlocks who certainly would not have known which fork to use at the James' dinner table.

"Oh Evie, if only you knew him, you'd like him" Zuelika said.

But deep down she knew that such a meeting would only have resulted in Joseph's sulky anger at being presented with living proof of his oppressor slave master's descendants, and in turn, Evelyn's attitude of superiority towards those Black people she considered inferior – which was the majority.

No, Zuelika knew that she never could have introduced those two....

"I feel better now," she said. "Let's join the others.

"If you're sure, darling," said Evelyn sarcastically. "We don't want any more dramatic scenes."

This bitch, this absolute bitch... Zuelika thought, as she followed Evelyn into the dining room, where the television still flashed its news pictures to the gathered guests. "I hate her. She only invites me to show off, but she is the biggest racist of all time."

Their return to the dining table was greeted with enthusiasm. Zuelika's hysterical outburst had come when dinner was almost over. Now John James was on the phone to his Jamaica office to find out more news.

John James had enough black blood in him to make him feel at home in Jamaica, his preferred home. But his skin and features were European and his African ancestry only served to give him a permanent tan and a curl into his graying hair. His ancestors had farmed sugar land in Jamaica for three centuries, and though much of their estates had been sold off in modern Jamaica, there still remained enough property to make him a rich Jamaican, as well as a rich English man.

Yet, Jamaica was too parochial for the James, and they preferred to live in London, where they had access to the beautiful people, of whom they considered themselves the First Couple.

Now as she resumed her seat, Zuelika was very aware that everyone was waiting for her next word.

"I've got to get to him immediately. But I've got to find out where he is. Thank God, he's still alive." Zuelika acknowledged that the facts of the news report were correct.

"Please, let me call Busha." John James moved over the phone and she punched the numbers of Busha's private number.

"We've been trying to find you, Zuelika," said Busha's worried voice on the other end of the phone.

"Right now, he's at Eden Island in a coma. Doctors and nurses around the clock. And security like crazy. I'm going down on my plane in three hours time. Get a cab and pick up some clothes on your way here."

"Oh Busha, you always know what to do, what to say." Tears streamed down Zuelika's cheeks again, this time of relief. "I'm ready right now. I don't need anything. I'll be right there."

And as she excused herself from the table and the house, one of the persons present slipped away to another room and made several phone calls.

In the office over the Embankment, a satisfied voice said on the phone:

"Well done. Assassination attempt successful. Throw the cat among the pigeons. Divide and rule. Show the savages that this is not easy to win. Our real killer is ready for him now, well trained and perfect. Stay in touch."

*   *   *   *

Joseph said that when he woke up on Thatch Island, he didn't know if he was in Heaven or Hell.

Thatch Island was the most special, most private and most luxurious of all Busha's palaces. Passing yachts and fishing boats, seeing it from the sea, thought it no more than a collection of native thatched shacks clustered together between the coconut trees of a small white sand island, and therefore avoided it.

But behind this carefully crude exterior was a luxury villa of black marble floors, wicker, mahogany and straw furniture, jacuzzi pools, expensive art, a music studio, video unit, and a kitchen equipped to turn out Italian, French, Chinese or Jamaican food at any hour of the day or night.

There was a master bedroom suite, and two guest cottages, and it was in one of these, in a bed under a glass skylight that let in the sun by day and the stars by night through the leaves of two overhanging coconut trees, that Joseph awoke.

Heaven was the place, Hell was his pain.

There was a nurse dressed in white sitting in a corner, but Busha must have picked her, for she had a punk hairdo and wore white ballet slippers. In the waking sleeps he endured for three days, he realized that doctors came and checked on him and went. He remembered what had happened.... that he was singing, and then there was pain... but he didn't know what else had happened.

Then on the fourth day he realized Zuelika was with him, for he woke up and saw her looking at him, then she burst into tears and said: "Thank God!" He tried to speak, to say "JAH", but found that the effort made him hurt, so he stopped and went back to sleep.

As the days passed, and he grew more healed, Zuelika moved the nurse out and took over her duties. She joked that her 'pay' was getting to sleep next to Joseph at nights, and hold him in the large soft bed with arms that she hoped held as much healing as they did love.

Joseph was grateful. The little boy inside him that longed for his mother to comfort his hurt, was glad for this warm woman's love.

Having assured himself that his most precious investment was still intact and mending, Busha had returned to London, leaving his girlfriend Suzie behind in the main quarters to keep in touch with him and run the house. Suzie was blonde and and Swedish, and said she was a model. She was on a diet that was so strict, all she talked about was food – meals enjoyed in expensive restaurants, delicatessens she liked to shop at, ice cream flavors – she made Joseph laugh, holding his wound against the pain of his laughter.

The other guest cottage was empty, but held the video library, so Joseph and Zuelika would often walk through the sand paths laid out in Japanese rock gardens that linked the villa buildings, and spend hours looking at old movies, musicals, cartoons, black films,documentaries and music videos.

There was a shelf of pornographic films too, and one afternoon, when Zuelika gone into the nearby sea for a swim, Joseph had put one into the VCR, but after five minutes he was so disgusted with himself for having allowed the awful images into his mind, that he swept the whole shelf onto the floor with a loud crash that brought Zuelika running back to say, with a laugh:

"One at a time – don't be greedy," and to laugh even louder as Joseph shouted: "Blood-klaat........fuckery......FIRE BUN SODOM!"

"Come cool off in the sea," Zuelika laughed, and for the first time since he was shot Joseph made love, soothed by the warm water lapping on a totally deserted white sand beach, easing his arm out of the sling that held his bandaged chest secure, and – more from the memory than from conscious thought – allowed Zuelika's love to over power him.

It had been three weeks since the concert.

Joseph's only emotion at his condition was anger and betrayal. He was bitterly, deeply hurt at what had happened to his effort to make Peace, to change the ghetto running's once and for all.

There were moments, alone on the bed staring up at the stars in the night sky, that he actually wept, sobbed bitterly as he remembered the night, and cursed between his tears at the partial destruction of his body.

Over and over, shaking his head, he asked "Why, why? Who, who?"

But there were no answers, and this made him more angry. He didn't even know which of his close group to trust, and after he regained consciousness, he accepted Bush's suggestion that he not allow any visitors to come to the island for a while. Zuelika had been an exception.

Now, he wanted answers, wanted to speak to his man friends, his idren. He felt dislocated, cut off from Jamaica. There was so much he wanted to talk about. He couldn't stand the not knowing. Ten days after he regained consciousness, he asked Suzie to get Busha to contact Mikey, his football-playing idren from Wareika, and Peter, and bring them to Thatch Island.

"Peter can't be found anywhere," Zuelika reported back to Joseph. "He's disappeared."

"How come?" Joseph wanted to know.

"We don't know – we trying to find out. But needless to say, every gunman and Rastaman who was at the concert has gone into hiding. A lot of people died you know. Three women were trampled to death. One had her baby with her, he died too. Four dead of gunshot wounds, one with a broken neck – he fell from the Stadium wall trying to get out. Every day the number of injured goes up – today it's 142."

Zuelika was tense.

"The press on the phone night and day asking where you are, and if you are dead or alive. Everybody wants an exclusive interview. Tropics PR people are going crazy, Busha says"

"But don't you worry about a thing," she continued." Anything you want or need- anything at all- Busha says to ask Suzie. She will make arrangements to fly Mikey here."

It took Suzie 18 hours from she first picked up the touch-dial phone, until Mikey was standing in front of Joseph, tired from the rush and anxiety of a jet plane ride from Kingston to Nassau, a charter light plane and then a motor cruiser ride to Thatch Island, but he was so glad and relieved to see Joseph, he hugged him and burst into tears of joy and sorrow at seeing his wounded friend.

Words, questions, burst from them.

"Bwai – me glad you no dead....me neva know wha happen to you..."

"How Jenny?" (Mikey's girlfriend, a backup singer for one of the groups who performed on the Concert) "She alright?"

"Some bruises; she had to jump under the stage to escape the bullets. How YOU?"

"Bwai, me tell you – gunshot HOT, HOT, me neva know sey bullet so hot, so. Then one of me ribs break from the fall. Bwai me haffi thank JAH she me alive at all."

"Me know. Man sey you dead. Them have to come on the radio to say you still alive, to stop the looting in the streets. Them bruk down New Kingston and Downtown. Politician beg for order, parson beg for peace, then they come on TV and tell them say you not dead. Is only then that the man-them stop. Man, a you control everything now. Them neva know say you so powerful."

Joseph shook his head in wonder. "Mikey, bwai, ME neva know say me so powerful."

There was a long thoughtful silence. Then Joseph gestured to a blue ceramic urn and said: "Build a spliff."

Mikey lifted the cover off the gracefully turned container, releasing the familiar fragrance of resinous herb. From its smell, they could tell it was the best sensei. Beside the urn was a matching flat dish with a pearl handled knife resting in a specially shaped place, while the back of the dish held a container for rolling papers.

"Bway – a-so them stylish, ya!" Mikey was impressed.

Joseph, used by now to some of the trinkets of the very rich, just shrugged.

"The ganja taste just the same. Roll it."

Mikey cut up the sticky leaves, rolled them into two large cones, and they lit them, exhaled a big cloud of sweet smoke, and meditated.

There was only one question Joseph wanted answered, but he so dreaded the answer,

"Wha' Niah Simon say?"

Mikey drew long on his spliff, looking intently at the tip, then removed it from his mouth and stared at the glowing fire.

Finally he spoke.
"Him say: Fire, hotter Fire."

Joseph flinched. The three words were almost like a death sentence, worse pain than the bullet wound.

Mikey continued: "Him say him tell you no fi do no show fi ghetto murderers. Him say a-now Rasta a-go feel it, and a-you

90

cause it." He paused. "Nyabingi a-go malice you if you go back a Jay-A, now. Them want fi show dem an' you is not the same thing."

Joseph thought of this, then sighed.
"Bwai, you just can' win. I do the show to make Rasta look good, and now is my head them a-look."

A thought occurred to them both. "You think is Niah order the shot for you at the show?" They considered this, then Joseph dismissed it.

"No, Niah wouldn't do no evil. He would just wait and see what JAH mek happen. An' like how JAH sen' a bullet for me, him feel say JAH act for him.

"Rasta, it look like say me can' go back a-Jamaica now. An' me no wan' stay here. It nice but me feel uncomfortable. Too much comfort. Bed too soft. Food too rich. Wha me fi do?"

Mikey thought for a long while. Their spliffs burned, giving off the fragrant incense into the cool evening air, stirring thoughts of consciousness and righteousness and up-fulness in their minds, their thoughts, their souls.

Mikey finally spoke.
"Come we go a-Ethiopia."

It was the best thing Joseph had heard for weeks. He felt as if all the confusion and pain of the past days had all been for this divine purpose- to give a chance to see his beloved Zion, free from obligations to record companies, families or friends.

"Mikey," he spoke with relief. "You are JAH-son himself. Help me set it up. Come we a go a-Ethiopia."

At last there was a purpose to sitting under the coconut trees, waiting for a bullet wound to heal enough for travel.

*　　　*　　　*　　　*

91

When Zuelika was telling me this coming part of the story, she was crying again, as she remembered it. That girl is so sorry for how she lost Joseph, she wished she could press the rewind button on that part of her life's tape.

Underlying the relationship between them both, was the fact that Zuelika was a star in her own right. Joseph was famous, true, but Zuelika was a celebrity of a more popular kind, the kind that is seen in gossip columns and on premier occasions, and at the right parties and night clubs. Her music got good reviews and she often guest-starred on TV programmes.

But she had to be constantly aware that she was, in her relationship with Joseph, first of all a woman, and a Rasta man's woman, which meant that... whatever her achievements or fame, she was basically intended to play a secondary role – if she could. For indeed it was always hard for her to fight down her Western woman ways, her acting and doing and thinking first and independently, rather than submissively deferring to her man first at all times.

She knew this was the role she should play, but she did not know how a wise woman plays this role without either giving over her independence and will, nor dominating her man and emasculating him by showing independence and will too obviously. She tried to learn how to be, and thought she had learnt, but she confesses sadly that it was losing Joseph that taught her how.

Even though she loved being with him, most of of all loved being the woman of such a special man, she resented the fact that he didn't love her "special-ness" specially; just expected her to be like an ordinary woman, living his life and pretending she didn't have a life of her own.

She smoked as much herb as he, and somehow it gave their relationship the air of Rasta King and Queen (especially because of the dramatic clothes Zuelika used to wear) which made Joseph a little uncomfortable, and made Zuelika feel unloved at times.

The Grammy Award show was special to her, because she had been nominated at last as a New Artist, and wanted to attend, even though she didn't think she had much of a chance of winning. At least she would be on prime-time TV worldwide – that was worth as much as winning, to her career.

But a large part of her wanted to stay with her man at this crucial time in his life, when they were so close together. She hope Joseph understood what it meant to her to be switching on the satellite-linked, 7 foot big TV screen in the video room, that evening, to watch the Grammy's with Joseph (and Mikey and Suzie and the Chinese chef, and the Jamaican guards) rather than actually being there in person.

Joseph was interested in seeing the show, too. It was one of his ambitions to win a Grammy for his works.

"Me a-go win one a dem, one day," he said proudly, settling back to watch from a comfortable, footrested armchair. Zuelika sat on a zebra-skin cushion on the floor, by his feet.

"Cho," she said, half laughing. "They not giving one to no Rasta." They all laughed at the sad joke, except Joseph, who just humped up his shoulders seriously.

The presenter, a clean-cut white American, announced nominees and winners in each category, introduced the stars of the music and film who presented each award. Dancers danced, singers sang, celebrities in the audience pretended they didn't see the TV cameras focused on their well-dressed selves.

Zuelika opened a bottle of dry white wine, offered Joseph some, which he refused, and then sat sipping it slowly from a thin goblet while the show unfolded. Every now and the she would point excitedly at some celebrity, or tell Joseph a story about another member of her entertainment clique. Joseph was not really interested, but watching the show with a big spliff was a good way of thinking, especially about his music.

He was able to ignore Zuelika, too.

"There's George!", Zuelika's cry drew his attention to the screen. On it was a tall slim brown man, with shiny black hair that had clearly been straightened. He wore a peach – coloured suit, pale green shirt and a big white smile..

"Hi George," Zuelika smiled, waving as if he could hear her. She jumped up excitedly. "I did a TV special with him in Los Angeles last month. He's fabulous."
She hugged herself.

George read out the nominations.

"And now, the nominees for Best New Artist, Female: ROSALYN EVANS (...the fat, familiar face of the gospel singer filled the screen, singing from her album's hit.); KIKI LAFONT...(the moody, sexy body of Kiki, her lush lips outlined in red mouthing her latest love song...) "and last but by no means the least," added George with a lecherous look on his face..."ZUELIKA!" Zuelika's video, showing her windswept peasant look, came on screen.

There was applause from the audience, and the camera picked up Kiki in the third row, dressed in black with gold shoulder pads and hat... the plump Rosalyn with a new hairdo that still didn't make her look pretty.... then it seemed to search for Zuelika, but did not find her...

"..and the winner is.... KIKI LAFONT!!"

The screen showed Kiki jumping out of her seat, the mink coat she had drapped across her shoulders falling carelessly behind her, her dress falling open to reveal a leg-revealing slit, and as she bent over to pass the others in her row, her obvious cleavage fell naturally forward. It only took her a minute to reach the stage and receive her Grammy, say her excited thanks. But for Zuelika and Joseph, it took her a lifetime. They watched silently as George Harris hugged and kissed Kiki, kissed her as if she was very special to him.

"I should have been there."

This time Zuelika's voice was angry.

She got up and poured some fresh wine into her glass, and sat down again without looking at Joseph.

"So why didn't you go?" Joseph asked the question in search of an answer, and waited, but Zuelika didn't answer.

"Why didn't you go?" he asked again. "You didn't have to be here." His voice was cold and sad.

She turned to him, and said the words she most regrets having said in her entire life.

"You're damn right. I've spent five weeks here nursing you and neglecting my own life, my career. You want to turn me into some kind of glorified maid, you want me to be just another of your women, never speaking, never having a thought. But I am just ME. I have my own life and I had it before I met you.

"My life is important to me. I've worked hard to get where I am, and I know if I had been sensible enough, I would have realized that unless you are a big star, you have to be present at such an event, or they think you don't want their award.

"And believe me, I wanted it. That girl Kiki, her music is not as good as mine, and she can't sing. All she has is big tits. I've been acting like I've retired, like I'm some kind of wife, or something. I must be crazy."

Joseph listened to her without looking at her, analyzing her voice and her words. Then with a heavy sigh, he took his arm out of the sling and moved it up and down.

He spoke softly, but with strength.

"You see me? Better now. Strong. Thank you for the nursing and for the loving. It's time for you to go back to your world, the world that is full of people like Face-man George and Kiki, the whore.

JOSEPH - A RASTA REGGAE FABLE

"Rasta is not for you. You will never see the light.

"Don't let me see you again."
And he got up and closed the door.

Zuelika immediately regretted every word, more than she had ever regretted anything she had ever done in her life. She ran to the door and began to beat on it, calling out to him.

"JOSEPH! JOSEPH! OPEN THE DOOR! I didn't mean it. Please open the door..."

But when her crying had turned to sobs, and then to self-pity, the compassion in Joseph made him say from behind the locked door: "When you ask permission to leave heaven, you're not allowed to change your mind."

She left the next day on the motor launch that brought the week's mail. She didn't know how very glad Suzie, Busha girlfriend, was to be the only woman on the island with Joseph. She did not intend to let pass an opportunity to know what it is like to sleep with a Rastaman.

*   *   *   *

While he waited, Joseph acted. First he got the Kingston office to send some presents to some friends of his.

Presents like money. $10,000 to Ras Jama, to build the library. A truckload of food and boat load of fish to the Elders at Bull Bay. And a surprising present: $10,000 to the building of the Ethiopian Orthodox Church in Kingston.

"Why?" Mikey asked.

"I go there one time. Is the only church I ever feel comfortable in." Joseph spoke softly. "Bamboo mek it, and all the idren are dreadlocks. I like to hear them chant. Them say the prayers in new, upfull way. It kinda humble without all that crying and death-business you find in the dead-Christ churches."

96

"What kind of church?" Mikey asked.

"You know. Those churches that worship the Christ dead on a cross. I know that Christ came to show us life, and life abundantly, so I can't worship in a church that is always reminding me of Christ dying – In the Ethiopian Church, they worship the Christ reborn, by showing us Mary and the Baby on the altar. Christ re-born as an Ethiopian Child, Selassie I."

Mikey snorted. "Cho!" he sounded disdainful. The Sons of Jacob movement of which Mikey and Joseph were members, looked down on membership of any organized church, especially one which was modeled on the rituals of the European church. "You a-go join church?"

"No. Me nah join nothing. But the Church deserves something out of the plenty I Father a-send I."
And the matter remained closed.

Joseph spent a lot of time reading and meditating on his Psalms.

"Blessed is the man and woman that walketh not in the ways of sinners."

Joseph laughed, when he thought about the effeminate walk of homosexuals. Then he looked into himself to see where his path had been sinful, even to cause the suffering he was now undergoing.

Was he being too satisfied with his fame and money? Was he letting it go to his head?
No, he could answer to both questions.

Was he doing his work? That Greater Purpose for which he had been placed on Earth.

That could not easily be answered. Job sufferings, he thought. The Father is trying me in the Fire to see if I can endure and get stronger.

97

Job sufferings.

JAH Father, I am truly tired of Job sufferings.
First my Father, then my young life.
Now this bitter, when it should be sweet. So much bitter.

Father, show me what to do. Show I Father.
Let the words of I mouth, and the meditation of heart I, be acceptable in Thy sight, O Lord FARI, I strength and I Redeemer.

He closed the Book, and then holding it between flat palms, held out as in prayer he let the well-used pages fall open to wherever they wished, seeking his blessing.

It was 1st Corinthians, that it fell open to.
He started reading.
He saw the message soon, as he knew he would.

> *"But God has chosen the foolish things of the world to confound the wise; and God has chosen the weak thing of the world to confound the things that are mighty."*

"BLOW! WOW!" The sound escaped his lips like gunshots.
"What a word the Father sen' I! Jah Father, you' heavy. You powerful."

Joseph could only shake his head and marvel at how mystically his question had been answered. Only from the word could come the word. Hold on, it said. Stay simple. Stay Rasta. Stay low. Remain as a sufferer, so that sufferers can still be one with you, and you with them. Cool out.

And praise SELASSIE I. MOST HIGH.
JAH RASTAFARI.

All of a sudden, he was impatient to be leaving.
He could see his real work was just beginning, and the gunshot was the Father's way of pointing him in the right direction.
Whom JAH loveth, him He chasteneth.

CHAPTER SIX

"And one of the elders said unto me, Weep not: behold, the Lion of the Tribe of Juda, the Root of David, hath prevailed to open the book, and to lose the seven seals thereof.
REVELATION 5: V.5

For Peter and I, Miami was just a stop on the way to Cuba, the destination of our Wareika Hill helicopter connection. The trip had been scheduled as part of his refuge from the Peace Alliance-- an alliance which seemed created to destroy its leaders. Peter was one of these, but he-- we-- wanted to stay alive.

Our temporary hosts were a group of white American hippies who had adopted the Rastafari trappings to assist them in their fight to legalize herb. I found this amazing, to say the least, to meet such people. In the few days we had were there, I had a chance to observe their lifestyle, and to see that they lived according to the same Biblical principles as other Rastafari. I admired the valiant battle they were fighting in America and Jamaica, to legalize the use of herb as a spiritual sacrament.

But frankly, the amount of money they appeared to have made from the herb, made me feel that perhaps their fight was not simply for Rastafari sake but for their own. Some big, expensive cars were parked in the yard, and they spoke of the acres of land they owned both in Jamaica and America. They also openly told us they did not approve of dreadlocks, or the worship of Selassie as the returned Christ, as they felt the Black Jamaican leader of their movement was in fact the returned Christ.

I didn't feel any oneness with these people. They made me feel like they alone had the true message-- these white people-- and we Black Rastas were just a bunch of fools who needed white men to teach them the right.

Time will tell, was all I could think to myself, as I watched them move about the big house. The five days we spent there seemed like five years.

Peter's attitude to them, however was different.

"It is good for our movement when the children of Babylon go against their society and support Rastafari. It gives Babylon a good look at itself, and it shows that there are some who will side with the way of right and truth, if only to save their own souls. At least these people don't mingle outside their race. What is happening is that those who want to destroy Rasta, are sending down white girls, specifically to mingle with Rasta and dilute the philosophy. That is far more dangerous than these guerrilla fighters of the herbal war."

Not a day too soon for me, we arrived in Havana. Our trip from Miami via Mexico City was taken on scheduled flights with documents that listed Peter as a trade unionist and myself as a secretary.

Now we were staying in a cottage at Santa Maria del Mar-- the pine-tree covered, white sand beach resort outside the capital, where brightly coloured houses had privacy among the trees. It was the most wonderful holiday that I had ever had-- days of rising early to fruit and a swim; then our tour guide would take us by car to tour a factory, a housing estate, an island school for Third World children, the monuments at a small restaurant in Old Havana, or visit the ballet or a cultural show in one of the many downtown parks.

Cuba was wonderful, and Peter-- whose Revolutionary Rastafari philosophy was at its heart a form Socialism-- was perfectly at home here. It was his philosophy which the Cubans were eager to discuss with him, and this they did in frequent, friendly conversations.

"We feel you could be a person who could advance our goals in Jamaica and the Caribbean," said Pedro Arriva-- the DGI man sent to accompany our life in Cuba. He lived with us in the cottage, and drove the car which took us around Cuba.

Cuba was so free. The people all looked proud and happy to be Cubans, and to be living in the Revolution.

I said this to Peter and he explained: "They are their own boss. They may be poor, and under pressure, but the country is theirs; no man owns them."

"But what about Russia? Doesn't Russia own them?"

"No," replied Peter. That alliance is made with their own free will. It is not an inherited system that was the cause of their existence and their problems. Marxism is the way they see as forward for them."

"You speak like a Socialist-- are you?" asked Arriva.

"I am Rasta," Peter answered him proudly, "and that was Socialism before Fidel Castro was born. Rasta showed how man-and-man should dwell together in love and sharing, when I&I lived in the camps of Dungle, where they dumped the garbage of Kingston. It was the only land where nobody didn't care if you captured it so I&I – who society consider the garbage---made our homes there as we had no homes, no land. Nothing, even though our fathers had built the city whose stinking garbage we were living on."

"Our Socialism is Communal-ism, living communally and sharing what I&I have. Working by the labour of our hands and minds to provide-- not just for our own-- but for the whole community; the children, the widows, the fatherless, the old, the sick and the well. THAT is true Socialism and that was our African Inity, long before Marx went to his German library and found the description of the African livity which had been recorded by European colonizers."

He smiled. "So, yes, Cuban brother, I am Socialist, if this is the way to describe what Africans have always been, and you are now striving to become."

Arriva sighed, as if he was still hoping this Black man would finally understand the Marxist way of thinking.
"But where are your economic theories of organization? How will your society be organized? Where is your PLAN?"

He threw up his hand in despair.

"I&I plan is the Bible," Peter answered, "the way of JAH laws. That is what I&I fathers, and fathers' fathers have used to organize our societies."

"You can't use a book of mystical fables to live your people's lives?" Arriva protested.

"Why not?" asked Peter. "You use a book which is truly fables, for Marx's theory can't work for Black people. We need to put our God and our racial history into whatever philosophy rules us. That is what Garvey emphasized, and he was right. Until we use Garvey as you use Marx, we won't be a nation or a race that lives in peace and respect, like Cuba.

Arriva considered this, then asked Peter. "What do you need God for?"

Peter laughed.
"JAH—our Father? What I need him for? Ha! Ha!
"I need Him to give I light, and water and food, and health, and happiness. Without Him, I'm just a leaf, living and dying on a tree without ever becoming a tree I-self."

And saying that he stood up, shook his locks from his tam and roared:

JAH! RASTAFARI!

Arriva smiled and shook his head.
Yes, Cuba was nice.

The country side looked just like Jamaica. The people were a little different, with their mulatto looks, but there were enough Black people to make us feel right at home. Blacks looked at us with more amazement than the average Cuban, who had never seen locks before, had never seen red-gold and green crowns, or a long skirt on a woman.

Some had heard of Rastafari, though, for often we would hear them whisper as we passed "Rastafari."

Peter asked Arriva daily when he would meet Fidel. Arriva would laugh happily.
"What are you going to say to him?"

Peter would get serious.
"I have a most important question to ask him. Tell him I won't leave until I have seen him."

Yes, we knew we would have to leave Cuba, though we wished we could say forever. Peter had to clear his name.

We were in Cuba, though, for the Carnival, when the grand seaside avenue, the Malecon, came alive with a parade of floats and costumed groups of incredible beauty and design, some three stories high, a night of music, fireworks, food, drinks and laughter.

We were filled full of happiness and spectacle as we watched the parade, and we were not surprised when we were swept up with the revellers of a giant float-- our clothes, for once, blending with the bright costumes around us.

Happy arms lifted us up on to the deck of the float, from where we watched the greater spectacle of the passing crowds. Then other arms pulled us along on the float's deck through a small doorway, into a cabin beneath.

There, to our amazement, sat Fidel smilingly chomping on a cigar, among a group of comrades. Smiling, Arriva stepped forward, shook his leader's hand with confidence, then presented Peter to Fidel, as I watched and listened.

"Thank you for your hospitality," Peter was quick to speak. "We have loved being here in Cuba."

The big man smiled, and did not wait for an interpreter. When he spoke, it was in English.

"I hear you have a question for me? What is it?"

Peter relaxed, and smiled back.

"I once read where you said the objective of the Cuban Revolution is to ultimately make man care so much for his brother man, that eventually the need for money as means of exchange will no longer be there...that man will be so united in equality of opportunity, equal satisfaction of need, that the competitive spirit will be replaced with the spirit of loving brotherhood. I think this is a noble objective."

Fidel smiled.

"My question is this: "Is this not the fundamental principle of Christianity, of a religious belief in God which, as a Marxist you do not recognize?"

Fidel smiled again, then leaned back in his chair, arms behind his head. He thought for a moment, turned to translate some of Peter's words to his colleagues, to await a response from one of them, before he spoke.

"I was brought up a Catholic, so I have been taught the principles of Christianity, and the laws of God. Even though I am Marxist, I can see that what is called the law of God is merely the law of man. It is the deep inner feeling we all have, to know what is good. THAT is the real Christ within us, that is the true Christianity, and you don't have to be Catholic or an Anglican or a Moslem or a Hindu, to understand that. As a Marxist, dedicated to relieving the suffering of all my people equally, I don't see any contradiction, or even any religiousness, in thinking the way I do."

Peter nodded, accepting this.
"I only asked," he said, "because what you said was so exactly what I feel."

Fidel smiled. "My Jamaican brother-- the same Supreme Spirit which guides you to seek solutions for your people in Rastafari, has led me to seek solutions for my people in Marxism. With such fundamental goodness in your ideology, I hope that the day soon comes when you will be able to put your solutions into practice in Jamaica."

"Well," said Peter, "if not in Jamaica, then certainly in some new promised land."

"Vaya con Dios, my young revolutionary brother." Fidel stood, embraced Peter in his bear hug, stretched out his hand to where I stood and shook it, then he turned and was gone, up out of the float and into the noisy, musical night.

*   *   *   *

"And now that you have spoken to Fidel, where do you want to go next?" asked Arriva, two days later, when the Carnival was just a happy memory.

"Ethiopia." Peter answered.

Arriva laughed. "Fidel bet twenty pesetas, that was your destination."

He smiled. "It's a long trip, you know. Seventeen hours by troop transport-- a plane load of soldiers getting drunker and drunker." He looked at me. Peter put his arms around me protectively.

"I'll miss you, and our chats," Arriva told Peter.

Peter smiled. "At least, you won't forget me."

*   *   *   *

Sometimes when Joseph and I talked during those heavyweight hours spent at the Debre Zeit Monastery, he would say that knowing Peter made him change his whole outlook on life, made the Joseph who was now arriving at Heathrow Airport, very very different from the person who had become a star, at the Lyceum 5 years before.

105

This time Customs was no hassle. Not only was Joseph well enough known by now to have fans among the people waiting outside, but now he was accompanied by Mikey dressed in full football kit- the only style he ever wore - and they also were being met by a white man who could have been their manager, instead of just Journalist Sam playing a game to earn them all the respect and speed needed from Customs and Immigration officials.

As they flopped laughing into the seat of a London taxi Joseph said, "Sammy -boy you earn your rights just by the laughs you give me. Them neva even search me bag! I wish I had a pillow full of collie!"

Sam laughed. "You can't get rid of me. I traced you to Busha's island, they told me you had left for London and it was easy to find your flight and meet it. I am not letting you go until I get my full story. I told you already."

"Well, bwai, me tell you say there is NO story. Me no know who shot me, an' me jus' a cool out a' London. Me nah do nuttin!" Joseph was clear.

"So you say," Sam persisted, "but where you are there's a story. And ROLLING STONE wants that story, so you are stuck with me."

London was its usual gray self, silent and aggressive with its cold stone buildings and gray ribbons of roads and highways.

Brown's Hotel on the border between fashionable Notting Hill Gate and the black ghetto of Ladbroke Grove, was the ideal place to stay. A converted mansion house, bright red tables and cushions, and lots of ferns and palm trees indoors...

Joseph's room was a small suite opening out on to a verandah beside the garden, filled with pink and lavender hydrangeas. Within distance was the Portobello Road where a dreadlocks could be right at home in the street market full of bananas, sweet potatoes, salt fish and dry coconut, as well as the wonderful variety of fresh vegetable and fruits, spinach, mushroom, cauliflower, apples and pears. There were the shops selling food for vegetarians; brown rice and tofu nuts. There were the shops selling Rasta colours clothing, and those selling patties and fried chicken.

Around the corner, off the Grove itself, was Tropic's main recording studio, where Joseph had laid down tracks for the Cubs first album. The Grove was, of course the best place in town to buy herb. And the best place to catch up on Rasta and Jamaican running's.

Joseph and Mikey spent some of the first few days waking late, and walking down to the Grove, past the outdoors barrows filled with fresh food, through the throngs of people, Black, White, Indians who stopped on the street or lounged on the sidewalk. It was early spring, and a pale sun warmed the air and made London look beautiful.

On the Grove Joseph was recognized often, for the sensational headlines had been published everywhere. He was not just another dreadlocks, but looked at with special awe and admiration. Soon the crowd pressed too close, and he disappeared into a taxi which Mikey sensibly hailed.

Most of what I know of Joseph's visit to London came later from conversations with Red Dread.

Red Dread was what they called "Black English", but he was truly a red-skin Black man. His mother was English, Cockney, poor, his father a Jamaican from the first wave of immigrants.
If he had shaved and trimmed, he could pass for a white with, called a nigger from his early youth in Bristol's ghetto.

Now he was a dreadlocks of 15 years growth, living in the London headquarters of the Research and Repatriation Committee, a very militant off shot of the Ethiopian World Federation. Joseph had met him backstage after his first Lyceum concert briefly, and remembered the meeting and their conversation.

"Remember I?" Red Dread asked him when Joseph entered to find him seated in the lobby of the hotel.

"Yes, yes. Love. How could I forget the Idren. Come let us reason. Better still, come we tour and reason."

Red Dread pointed outside to an old, but roomy Jaguar car already nearly full of long-dreaded Rastas. Joseph and Mikey looked at each other happily, and turned and stepped into the car.

"A dem man me did a tell you about Mikey. Dem a de revolutionary Rasta inna London," said Joseph.

"How you mean 'dem'? "What about the Sons of Jacob?" Mikey was quick to defend his tribe.

"Well the Sons of Jacob deal with the gathering of the faithful, but the R and R Committee deal with the war against Babylon."

"So what onoo a-gwan with nowadays?" Joseph asked.

"Same running's – writing letters to the Queen and the Prime Minister telling them it is them moral and central obligation to repatriate Rastafarian. Collecting as much information as we can on Africa, Ethiopia and her people, then and now. And quaking the wicked system every chance we get wid FIYA!

The car load of dreads rocked with laughter for a while.

"Who shot you, Joseph?" Red Dread asked directly.

"Iya, me no know. Dem say is one boy whe 'run' way lef Jamaica. But him a mi fren. Why him would wan' kill me? Tell me. I know you bredren know everything?"

"You mean Peter? Peter is in Cuba now hiding from life. But he is not your killer, your killer embraces you." Red Dread was serious.

"You pose a riddle?" Joseph was quiet.

"Not really. But you can solve the riddle. Come we go smoke some herb."

They drove across London, through residential suburbs, town centers, highways and back streets, until they finally came to a stop outside a derelict building in a South East London ghetto.

Stepping through a broken gate, a dirty and unpainted door and into a large room, Red Dread gave the greetings.

"RASTAFARI!"

He was answered by a room full of dreadlocksed brethren and sisters, staring seriously and intently at Joseph.

"Hail up, Brother Joseph", "One Love JAH-son," "Selassie I reign," were among the greetings he received from the gathering, seated on narrow wooden benches, still in their coats for warmth in the rotting, damp house. Beneath their outer garments, each wore clothes of khaki decorated in red, gold and green. Even the sisters wore khaki skirts, some adorned with patterned material. An army in waiting.

Apart from that, there was silence as the group waited to begin the strict ritual of their week's meeting. First the singing of the solemn hymn of Garveyites and Rastafari:

> *"Arise, Arise, oh Negus I."*
> *Who keeps Ethiopia free*
> *To advance with truths and rights*
> *To advance with Love and Light."*

Then the reading from the "Philosophy and Opinions of Marcus Garvey" and the reasoning on the reading. Then, after news and notices, Red Dread stepped forward and began.

"Love, Idren. You all know Brother Joseph. Not just as the reggae star but as the Rastaman son of Selassie, JAH himself."

There were answers of approval

Joseph stood up and spoke. "JAH Rastafari, Selassie I. Blessings in the name of I and I father. Well, I really didn't come here to make a speech, so tell me what I can do."

"So why you come to London?" a brother asked. "You a do a show, or or the man in hiding?"

"No. I am here to get a visa to travel to Ethiopia. As a matter of fact, how onoo find me?" Joseph spoke.

"The R and R Committee knows everything. One of I Idren spen' the time at Heathrow Airport seeing who comes in from Jamaica. If British Security does it, shouldn't we? The importance of security is not lost on I and I idren."

Joseph was impressed.
"You know I've heard about you idren; but man-an man say you not official. Whey onoo really a deal with?"

"Well, brother Joseph, I & I a deal with Repatriation, same as the I. I & I born of the beas' so I & I desire to trod to Zion is deep, deep. I & I, the Black Rasta of England, born and grow in the hatred that was the energy that powered slavery and colonialism. I and I feel it. I and I know it. So I and I must dread, for I and I serious. And taking it serious, we write letters regularly to the Queen and the Prime Minister and people like that, pointing out our righteous claim for repatriation."

"Bwai, onoo good. Me know sey a no easy work." Joseph shook his head. "How you live?"

"On the State!" There was a roar of laughing approval from the group. "We feel that it is our duty to let the Englishman feel it in his pocket for keeping us here. We collect the dole, we get students grants, we live in council house-- we give the social system full use."

Joseph laughed nodding approval.

"You see like how you a-trod to Ethiopia, I would a-like to come too, to see the place. Carry me with you, nuh?" Red Dread was serious. Joseph laughed, it was so direct.

"I would have to check it out. But the man have a vibe I man like."

"Whe the man a do fi Ethiopia?" another man asked.

"How you mean?" asked Joseph.

"Well, de famine....the political oppression, the church?"

"Well, I-man chant Selassie I Christ, you know."

"There is more to be done," the brother continued. "The political work is vital. We must not pretend that the world does not exist, and we must confront the systems with defiance, and with our message, and our presence."

"Me no like deal with politics," Joseph shrugged off the weight of that. "I am jus' a ordinary man, I-a. Jah father sen' I for one work, and then sen' you for another, a-so we haffi trod it."

"How are you going to get your visa? It hard, you know. Some idren try all the time to go, but the man-them no want no Rasta inna dem country."
Another dread had spoken.

"We'll go through Tropic Records. They can't stop us." Joseph ended the problem. The meeting, too was over, people were leaving.

"How can I hear some irie music in this town? Me can' hear no reggae." Joseph commented.

"If you wan' hear music, you haffi go a Sons of Jacob dance," said one of the brethren.

"Where is that happening?" Joseph asked.

"Come we check nuh? Get some good herbs too, and some good ital food." They piled into the big old car again and set off.

At the central cross road of Brixton, the darkest black ghetto, some primitive signs of black business thrived. The stores selling wigs, hair straighteners and beauty aids, the electronic shops of radios, TV, and some records; the black bookshops for tourists and intellectuals but hardly locals, the fabric stores with bright colours and tropical prints. In between them, and with equal darkness, the stores where whites sold the necessities of life to the black population-- fish shops, meat shops, vegetable shops, bread shops, liquor shops-- the greatest prosperity going, as always to the master race.

The nearby market existed to provide black London with the foods of their homelands, to ease the pain of home sickness. Yet even this heart of what should have been the closest echo of their homeland, was dark and ugly, an advertisement of the poverty of the people it served.

"You know," Joseph said, "I don't know why I feel I come to mash down Babylon, but when I see brethren and sisters and mothers and daughters live in a place like this, I feel I have to do everything I can to bring us out of this rass claat darkness into a place like Africa." He shook his head.

"You know, I see us all standing in the sun, wearing clothes that show how kings and queens bodies should be clothed-- not squeezed into these western dresses and pants and shirts and suits. Boy, when I think about our colours, our reds, our golds, our browns, our purple, our royal greens...boy...How we ever find ourselves trapped in a shit place like this, eeh?" Joseph wailed in pain.

"How are we going to come out, when most black people you see around you don't know they are in pain; when most of them are glad to be here in this hell, think that because they are being paid to feed and house themselves to make England greater, they are not still as much slaves as on the plantation. They think this is all the happiness they can ever have in life!"

112

"No one ever show them Africa's great past, or the possibility of it ever coming again. All they ever hear about Africa is negative, full of ridicule, or war or famine." He punched his fist into his other hand.

"They don't want to go there. They prefer to work to build the white people's cities, than to build cities of our own. Is these people I songs are for," Joseph continued gently. "I songs of freedom, to free their minds. One day the chains will be broken."

"JAH know, Rasta, JAH know." Red Dread echoed.

They came to a stop outside a small shop brightly painted in red,gold and green, with African and Rasta artifacts in the window.

"Wait here," said Red Dread and disappeared inside, returning to the car with another Rastaman beside him.

"Hail Brother Joseph. I-man is Ras Zebulun. Glad to sight the I. Me hear so much about the brother's work, I-man give thanks. Well, I-man proud to present the I with an invitation to attend I&I Sons of Jacob dance this Saturday, livicated to the Son of Levi. I hear-say you a-step to Ethiopia, and the presence of the I would be most welcome at our gathering. It will give the I the right vibe to step forward to Zion."

Joseph smiled broadly, "Cool, I. One Love."

"This is the best draw in Brixton," Zebulun continued, and Joseph felt the handful of herb that was pressed into his hand with the handshake that accompanied the formal introduction-- a transaction no one else could see on the crowded, dangerous street.

Joseph was glad to be driving out of Brixton, back to the relative haven of Ladbroke Grove.

*   *   *   *

The good draw was just finishing two days later, it's soft green smell floating over the flowers in the very English garden of Joseph's hotel. The spring sun warmed the verandah on which Joseph and Mikey sat, their ears covered with stereo headphones on which they listened to the music of other reggae and African artists.

"Call Tropic again, Mikey." Joseph stirred himself. "Ask them about the visas."

"Bwoy, me no like chat to them gal down at Tropic. Them go on like dem nicer than I. Some of them. The res' of them a-beg me fi carry herb come for them. Me no want no white gal. And me no understan' the man-dem when them chat. A-you to phone them about the visas. A-you a' the superstar."

"Visa, what visa?"
It was Sam the journalist.

"You mother never tell you to knock before you come into a room?" Joseph took out his anger at Mikey on Sam, who simply laughed.

"I knew I'd get a story if I stuck around. Where are you going? I can get you a visa to any country in the world."

For a moment there was silence, then Mikey said: "How about Ethiopia?"

Sam laughed. "Oh, so that's where. No problem. No problem at all, man."

Mikey was angry. "Let us see if you are just pure chat. For four weeks, we have been waiting here for visas to Ethiopia, which Tropic assured us before we left Bahamas, would be ready when we got here. The Embassy man-dem won't say what is the hold-up."

Joseph quieted him. "If you can do it as you say, I'll give you the exclusive story that Joseph Planter is going to his homeland."

114

Sam laughed out loud. "I don't come cheap, my brother. If I get you the visas, I want to come with you on your trip. THAT'S the story I want." He waited.

"A whitey! Come with I&I Black idren to I&I Zion! You must be crazy!" Mikey exploded with outrage.

Sam laughed louder.
"You want your visas?"

Mikey moved across the room as if he was going to hit Sam. Just in time, Joseph put his hand between them. "That's a fair deal. You can come, if you can get us the visas. We need three, four including yours." He turned to Red Dread. "You can come with us."

Sam shot out his hand. "It's a deal," and pretended not to notice when Joseph didn't shake it. Instead he just sat down beside the phone and asked the operator to get him first ROLLING STONE Magazine's New York office and, after he had a brief chat with someone there whom he informed he was following a Joseph Planter story to Ethiopia, then asked the operator for the Ethiopian Embassy in London.

"Hello, Hello." His American accent was very pronounced, it seemed.

"Who is that speaking? I want to speak to the Colonel in charge. Mengoostoo? Oh, he's in Ethiopia! Well give me the next best man....I'm Sam from ROLLING STONE, the magazine of the richest business in the world-- show business.

"We're doing a story on good countries to make music in, and we want to send a journalist-- myself and four musicians to Addis Ababa to interconnect with the Ethiopian culture ... yes, meet the musicians, learn the music history, bring a gift for famine relief, sightsee ... Yes, right away. We have the musicians under contract, and everyday we wait it costs us US $8,000 in fees and payments .... anything you can do to get it speeded up ... yes, I'll be there myself in the morning to pick them up.,,,

"Thanks, Colonel. Thanks."

He turned, laughing to the room."Every country in the world wants entertainment magazine publicity. Now you guys owe me."

He took off his glasses and wiped them, then from his camera bag, full of so many pieces of equipment, he opened one camera case and dumped a whole heap of sweet bud sensimilla on the bed.

"This should hold you guys while I pack and get the tickets from Tropic. How much cash do we need in Travellers Cheques?"

With a smile, the a whoop of joy, Joseph dived on the bed, closely followed by Mikey. As they grabbed at the tight buds, flung them up in the air, threw them at each other, celebrating the fact that at last their magical trip was on.

"JAH, wonderful, beloved, Selassie I – truly, thou art mighty!" Joseph exulted. "Come we chant a Psalms of thanks! JAH is I&I Light and I&I salvation, who shall I fear? JAH is the strength of I&I life; of whom shall I be afraid." He was shouting joyously.

Joseph started tapping a drum beat on the bedside table, Red Dread joined him, and the growing noise brought the beat of the feet of the four warriors lounging in the lobby waiting, and who joined in the chanting, the laughter, the happiness, which seemed to continue and flow over, until two of the hotel receptionists had come to see what the matter was, and stayed.

And the some guests checking out had heard that Joseph Planter was in the hotel, and joined in, and the enjoyment continued as a tape was put on the stereo, and drinks were ordered and the room grew fuller and happier and noiser.

Joseph felt he needed somewhere to think, stepped outside into the garden, and eventually found himself walking around the London streets, thinking, until by the time he returned to the hotel the place had fallen asleep.

He was not there when the switchboard operator had called the room to tell them to stop the noise, and he didn't hear what Mikey said to her:

"Disturbing WHAT Peace? I&I make Peace. I&I chant I&I Holy Father JAH RASTAFARI! SELASSIE I!" (A chorus of RASTAFARI! echoed from all the Rastas in the room) "and bring Blessings even on you. So ease your noise, woman and wait for the PEACE that passeth all overstanding."

The roar of laughter, war cries and shouts of JAH which followed, so angered the switchboard operator, that she decided to do what the man who called her yesterday had asked, and write a report on the 'goings-on' at the hotel while Joseph Planter stayed there.

CHAPTER SEVEN

*"Oh Peaceful King of Peace, Jesus Christ, grant us thy peace
and confirm unto us thy peace, and forgive our sins and make
us worthy to go out and come into our homes in peace."*
Anaphora of the Apostles, Liturgy of the Ethiopian Orthodox Church.

The chimes of the church bells mixed with the clang of goat
horns, as the jeep carrying us passed to let a flock across the
road. The shepherd was draped in white cotton cloth, and wore
a wool shawl across his shoulders.

So here we were in Ethiopia. Thanks to Cuba and JAH.

"Frankly, we would like you out of the country as soon as
possible," said the official in Addis Ababa who confirmed our
visas. "The Selassie of your myth was very different in reality.
The people of Ethiopia are glad he has gone. They have seen a
better life since."

Peter did not react.
"We are here to visit our Jamaican brothers and sisters at
Shashemane, but I hope we will be able to sightsee as tourists.
We hope to get to Aksum, and maybe Lallibella."

The official looked at our crown-covered locks.
"No, no. Your pass is restricted to the road to and from
Shashemane, and Addis. Good day, and I hope your stay will be
short."

In the street outside his office, we looked around for our next
move. Suddenly a small voice beside us said "Rastafari." It was
an Ethiopian youth, who called with his finger from a narrow
street. We followed him where modern streets became streets of
yesterday's history, where Old Ethiopia had not yet disappeared
under the red and black banners of Marxism. We found
ourselves in a street market and following the boy through the
noisy pathways, through the piles of food, vegetables, fowls and
firewood, we turned a corner and saw a small shed. Outside sat
an old man.

Seeing us, he smiled a bright, surprised yet happy smile, in a face that was typically Ethiopian – oval, red-berry brown in colour, with dark, red-brown lips, and oval, soft eyes looking out from deep eye-brows. He gestured us to sit, and to our surprise, opened his shama cloth wrap to reveal a pouch, out of which he poured a priceless clatter of silver crosses of the Ethiopian Church.

Their special beauty was not just in the fine filigree, or the solid silver workings, which were beautiful enough. Their beauty was their design. The tips were crossed again, and then the cross was further decorated with curls, angles, even the Star of David intertwined, reminding of the linkage between the Ethiopian Church and the line of David through Solomon.

Turning to the youth who produced from inside the shop a small Amharic-English dictionary, the old man managed to convey to us that he was one of the warrior Rases who had fought with the Emperor's army in the battle against the Italians. The old man said it was good to face the enemy with a lion-mane head-dress that gave him the countenance of a lion, just as warriors ate raw meat like lions.

He had told the story to his children and grandchildren with pride, and this boy – his youngest grandson, had seen our locks and brought us to him, believing we were warriors from his grandfather's stories. Warriors, yes we were, but of a different kind, we tried to explain, but the dictionary only seemed to work one way.

Then Peter said: JAH! RASTAFARI! SELASSIE I!

"Oh-ho!" said the old man. "Ras Tafari. Selassie I! Come with me."

His finger beckoned us into the shop. And lifting up a curtain on a wall, which covered the secret shrine, he revealed a portrait of His Imperial Majesty Haile Selassie I seated with his family. What a wonderful sight this was to greet us. Despite what the official had said, not all the people were glad he was gone.

The Emperor was smiling in the photograph, which I had never seen him do in a photo before. I looked closer at it, and could see that he was smiling because his little dog was standing up on his back legs, front legs in the air, and you see that he was smiling because he had told the little dog to stand up and it had obeyed. It made me see a whole new side to this quiet dignified Emperor, a gentle man who could rule a kingdom and rear a family of princes and princesses, but also take time out to play with his dog.

Peter opened up his wallet, and showed the old man the picture of the Emperor he always carried of H.I.M in army uniform, and the old man's eyes opened wide. Speaking suddenly in a voice that was strong like a mature man, he spoke some words at us, and finally placed the crosses and the pouch in Peter's hand.

We looked at the grandson for translation, but all he said was: "He is saying: You are my family. This is your house." We looked around the small shed, wondering if the old man was inviting us to make ourselves at home in this small room with the holes in the wall and the dirt on the floor.

"No," we said. "We can't take these." And we tried to return them to the old man, but the grandson again translated the elder's words: "You are my family. This is your house," and pressed the crosses harder into Peter's hand and repeated "Ras Tafari Selassie I." And we understood that the old man meant that we were the children of the warrior he had been for Selassie, and deserved to inherit the wealth that had reminded him of his days of glory.

He bowed, placing his fingertips to his lips, and we realized it was time to go, for each moment we stayed endangered the safety of these two people. I couldn't help putting my hand on the elder's shoulder, and I knew by his smile that he did not mind me giving him a kiss on the cheek.

Did he know how mystical an experience he had just given us? Did he know or understand what Selassie or Rastafari meant to us?

Or was it just an unusual incident happening to two unusual people in a strange land?

No, nothing was strange in Ethiopia. And nothing that happened to us ever happened by chance. All is part of the Father's plan, and because we pray to HIM and meditate on his teachings, we are able to realize that He is driving the car we call Life, and I&I are only the fortunate passengers looking at the view, and hopefully learning to drive like JAH, so that we can become qualified for the ride called Eternity.

"Put these in you bosom," Peter put the crosses in the pouch and I placed it securely, where its weight reminded me of its presence. Crosses, like photos of the Emperor, were banned by those who now ruled Ethiopia.

"Where are we going to go, after Ethiopia?" I asked Peter. "We can't keep on running forever, trying to hide."

"Girl, I don't know. But the Father JAH will show us the way. He won't leave I&I. Chant a Psalm in my ear, let me hear some peace."

I leaned back on his arm and spoke one of the twelve Psalms I knew by heart, so that even without a Bible I was not without prayer. The words: *"Hear I when I call, oh JAH of righteousness; for Thou hast enlarged I when I was in distress. Have mercy on I&I and answer I prayers...."* were part of a powerful prayer Psalms. I spoke it four times, so that we could use the power of four to enlarge and make our inward prayer of that moment reach our Mighty Father.

We were so far from home, so alone in the middle of people, so visible and yet so open to disaster. Only our faith in the Father Selassie was keeping us afloat, making us go forward, as if we knew the way and knew what we were doing.

Indeed we did know the way, and also where we were going.

Upward, we hope to see the Father's face.

A rainbow came out the sky, and we noticed it because the other passengers in the little bus ceased their chatter and started pointing out the window and moving across the aisle to see it. It was on our side of the bus, so we looked for a while, like everyone else.

All of a sudden, the bottom half of it disappeared, leaving only the red, green and gold of it. I swear it

It was unbelievable. I looked at Peter and he looked at me, with our eyes wide open, and we burst out laughing and Peter let out a:

JAH! RASTAFARI!

And the whole bus turned to look at us, just in silent amazement. And then they started laughing too, and babbling in their language, and a woman came over and touched my crown and a man Peter's, so Peter took off his crown and shook his locks, and the shock and laughter at the sight of his locks flying had everyone falling over, still laughing, and the disorder of it all carried us the rest of the way to Shashemane, so that by the time we got off the bus, we were laden down with food and cheese and two baskets and a pair of chickens and even a tin pot, all given to us by these people.

It was a lovely homecoming.

Needless to say, Shashemane was the last place we expected to see JOSEPH.

*   *   *   *

"Why didn't you tell me he was here?"
Zuelika screamed at Busha down the telephone line.
"You bastard! You bastard!"

"Zuelika, darling you didn't ask," Busha slammed down the phone.

122

Tropic's office was buzzing with activity and anxiety. Around the circular table sat the senior executives of Tropic and their assistants, their faces either gloomy or worried.

"That damn woman." Busha growled. Noticing surprise on his secretary's face he corrected: "Not Zuelika. The damn receptionist." And looked at the paper in front of him again.

It was a Sunday paper, the kind that appeals to those people with bad personal lives and experiences, who want to hear scandals about others than themselves.

"RASTAFARI CULT LEADER IN DOPE ORGY" was the headline of a story, in which anger and imagination had caused a woman to declare as fact what was nothing but a lie that she could only have made up. She told of 'sex orgies' and round-the-clock use of ganja and 'other drugs' by Joseph and his friends at the hotel where she was a receptionist. She said it had caused guests to complain and to check out.

Worst of all, they printed a photo of Joseph clowning with a smile and a spliff, and beside that an old photo with Zuelika in a very short skirt from the minidress era, making her look both sexy and ridiculous at the same time.

"TIME was going to do a story on him," said the PR man. "Now their doing Bruce Springsteen instead."

"Who?" several eyes focused on him.
"Never mind."

"I was planning for him to do two big shows in America after he came back from holiday," Busha explained. "That Black American market is ready for him now, but this scandal...." Busha shook his head.

From the corner of the room, a figure uncurled itself from a pile of cushions, rose up and stretched the stretch of a man just waking from sleep. and pushed a lock or two back up into a tattered tam.

It was Toto, Tropic's pet Rasta, a man who knew full well his freedoms, and limits, as window dressing for this elaborate machine created to sell one of the valuables of Jamaican culture.

"De foreign press...a them make Joseph, so them a-show you say them a-go destroy him. An' them a-try destroy him by making him look like a criminal and a sexualist. Dem have the power."

"But JAH-JAH stronger than them. A HIM you must fret bout."

Busha thought about this statement for a moment or two, and then realized that he could never understand it. "Toto, you lose me when you speak in that Rasta mumbo jumbo,, but I just hope Joseph's guardian angel JAH can change such a big negative into a positive." Busha slammed down the paper.

*   *   *   *

"Zuelika, will you calm down? You're becoming very tiresome."

Evelyn James pushed back a forelock of her shoulder length hair from her forehead, with a well manicured hand that included a diamond-studded cigarette holder.

"I didn't even know he was here." Zuelika wailed. "This dirty rag is implying that I was part of his orgies, and I didn't even know he was here! I would have been camping on his doorstep begging him to let me in, if I had known."

"Well, he seem to have had enough company, dahling." Evelyn was cold.

"Women always flock him. What do you expect? He's a superstar, and very sexy, like a lion waiting to leap, but yet he is so full of love...."
Zuelika burst into tears.
"He doesn't even know what an orgy is."

"Oh, for heaven's sake..." Evelyn got up.

"And how did they get that damn picture. It was from a stupid fashion show I did years ago. It makes me look like a whore!"

Zuelika's tears flowed faster.

The phone rang.

"Go into the bathroom and wash your face. Your mascara's running," Evelyn commented as she reached for the phone. "That must be the caterers..... I need my thoughts together to speak to them...go, use my dressing room."

Zuelika got up, wiping her eyes and sniffing. She found the large living room doors, opened and closed them and walked down the long corridor to the large dressing room adjoining the James' master bedroom.

Then she remembered the guest bathroom contained a tray of her favourite brand of Guerlain soaps and creams...a nice little luxury of the James' house. She would go back through the living room quietly so as not to disturb Evelyn. The brass latch on the living room door only made a soft clunk, as she pressed it, and she was just about to go in when she heard:

"Yes .... Ethiopia ... place called Shema – something....I don't know ... Okay, I'll try..."

Zuelika's gasp made Evelyn James turn around.
She quickly tried to cover up.

"Don't forget the courgettes....the courgettes."

But Zuelika had jumped across the carpet onto a hassock in front of Evelyn, and onto her like a cat screaming:

"You bitch! You stinking two-faced, white bitch! You're selling out Joseph. The picture of me in the papers....I gave you one! You bitch! What do they pay you? Haven't you got enough money?"

125

She pulled and scratched and fought, and Evelyn's cries brought the fat Jamaican maid running, who with cries of 'Good behaviour, please' begged the women to stop, pulled them apart and then withdrew behind the kitchen door to listen, they well knew.

Wth a hiss, Zuelika said: "I'm going to find him and warn him."

Evelyn brushed down her cashmere sweater, pushed back her hair and said: "And then what? What will you tell him? That you chat so much you gave away information about him, that someone told someone else."

She was in full swing.

"And what can he do then? Bring the Rastaman army to burn down Babylon with me in it? Ha! Ha! Ha! Go run to you stupid little Rastaman, if he will have you. Go to your stupid little cult of dirtiness and madness and ganja. It mash you up already and it will mash you up again."

She stood up.

"Now get out of my expensive house, Black girl, and don't ever come back here again."

Zuelika stood up, shook her fluffy gold curls around her head, smoothed her jeans and jacket and picked up her bag.

"You know, Joseph once read me a part of the Bible, which is really appropriate for bitches like you who think your artificial beauty will last forever." Zuelika spoke seriously.

"It says that"....*it shall come to pass that instead of sweet smell there shall be stink; and instead of a girdle a rent; and instead of well set hair baldness, and instead of a stomacher, a girding of sackcloth; and burning instead of beauty."* Isaiah prophesied of what is in store for you, and I'll be around to see your wrinkled face when the prophecy is fulfilled."

"For sure, darling," Evelyn laughed.

And while her head was thrown back in that laugh, Zuelika spat fully into Evelyn James' face, before rushing out of the front door into the clean air, where she felt like a brand new person, tougher, stronger, and for the first time knowing her destiny and the work she must do.

As you know, Zuelika is dreadlocks now, locksed up that pretty golden mane, and started singing some heavy reggae blues. It's a brand new look and a brand new career, but she is sticking to it. She says the locks are for Joseph.

CHAPTER EIGHT

"But ye are a chosen generation, a royal priesthood, an holy nation, a peculiar people; that he should shew forth the praises of HIM who hath called you out of darkness into HIS marvellous light light."
1 EPISTLE OF PETER, Chapter 2, V.9

Shashemane is not all what you would expect. You know, you hear how it is the center of fruitful gardens where the food that grows there gets the highest prices in the markets, and you know that the Emperor gave the land as a gift to Black people of the West for their support of Ethiopia in the war against the Italian invaders, and you expect, well, something strong and irie, and Rasta.

But it is just a clearing on a hilltop with four one-room board houses and one half-finished concrete block building that is the school and hospital and everything. In fact, it looks a lot like a corner of Wareika Hill.

As we came walking along the road, some people sitting on the steps called out to those inside, and about fourteen people and children came out to welcome us silently, and waiting. A gray-haired man stepped forward....

"Peace and love in the name of I Father, JAH Rastafari," said Peter.

"Peace and Love," replied the elder. "Welcome to Shashemane. You are the two thousand, seven hundred and eighty-seventh Rastafari to come to I&I community. Come. You have arrived at a good time. We have special visitors. But let the introductions wait until you have washed and refreshed yourselves from your journey."

The elder turned and led us down a dirt track around the dwellings to a larger building at the end of the track. Just as we reached it, two dreads came out of the door.
It was Joseph, and Mikey.

The amazement on all our faces was incredible. To meet up with Joseph here, of all places-- in the middle of nowhere, yet the center of our common universe.

For Joseph, the shock was double, for standing in front of him was the man who it was said was his would-be assassin. But, as he later told me, just one look in Peter's eyes made him realize how false an accusation that was.

With a yell, Peter rushed him and hugged him like a child in his big arms, lifting Joseph's smaller body off the ground in his happiness.

"You know it wasn't I," Peter said, when he put Joseph down. "Me know say a never you, but now I know for sure," Joseph replied, "For JAH couldn't mek you and I buck up here."

"Me glad say you no dead," Peter said with seriousness. "If I didn't come here and see you, I wouldn't know say you alive at all."

"Where have you been, man?" Joseph asked.

I put down my backpack and, leaving Peter to fill Joseph in on our experiences since the night of the Concert, I asked one of the sisters to show me water. She told me they carried water from a nearby spring, but she would give me some of hers. In the days to come I was to find myself living Wareika Hill life again, carrying water on my head. What a way everything goes around in circles. That's why the Father says a true believer is happy whether they are in a palace or under a tree.

Because we had arrived, Joseph's posse of himself, Mikey, Red Dread and Brother Naptali all slept under a tree that night to give Peter and I privacy of the building for our first night at Shashemane. I made a fire outside the back door and cooked some peas stew and some taff-- the grain that only grows in Ethiopia, which the same sister who gave me the water brought me some of.

By the time it was ready, the Idren-dem had made a big fire outside in the clearing and stretched some canvas over their sleeping gear and were drumming and singing Nyabingi chants with big smiles on their faces and big spliffs in their hands.

Needless to say, the food was just gulped down as the man-dem talked and talked and laughed and reasoned about things that happened to us since the night of the concert.

And it was good to get a "Come hug me up, nuh, Sister Shanty," from Joseph, who grabbed me by the shoulders and gave me a good hug and kiss on the forehead. "Good to see the sister. The vibes always get peaceful when the sister is around. It's great to be back amongst I family."

Peter brought out the crosses the old man had given him; he told them all the story, and allowed each man to choose a cross for himself, giving me the ones that remained for safe-keeping.
They turned to other subjects, and I found this a good moment to go and make a sleeping place ready, so that when Peter came he would find our bed roll in a corner, made private by a long piece of wrap cloth hung over the open doorway, and a candle burning beside a small cone of incense. And when he came in later, he roused me by asking for his Bible and when he found it in the luggage, he placed it beside the candle and incense and opened it at Psalms 133.

"Behold how good and how pleasant it is for idren to dwell together in I-nity" he read, in his soft, deep voice. And when he was silent on his knees, and I knew he was praying, I said my prayer with him, that this night of union between I and I King-man, God and Goddess, would be the one to bring forward I&I God Child.

The sweet love look in Peter's eyes when he turned to me, made me feel that if a child was produced by only the highest ecstasy of love, then this should be the moment of our child's conception.

*   *   *   *

The Shashemane people were peaceful and nice, regular Rastas. But there was one thing that we all noticed, and Peter asked the man: "Why don't any of you carry locks? Aren't you Rasta?"

"Body lice," was his simple answer. "When we came here, we realized we could only deal with what was essential. We discovered that locks was not essential."

Joseph said: "I asked them, and got the same answer."

But one man around the fire said:
"I never locksed. I was one of the first beard-man, and in those times we never locksed. Some of Howell's men at Pinnacle locksed, which was the beginning of the locksing. But us other man-dem, we wore our beards and combed our hair. We didn't cut it but we comb it. Sometimes we would wear a cap, like an officer's cap, like Mr. Garvey's Officer Corps used to wear. Is like the locksman-dem was another tribe of Rastafari, because remember the Emperor we worship did not carry locks as a man, though he did as a child."

"So what made you come here to Shashemane?" Red Dread asked.

"Well," said the man whose name was Isaac, "I was living in England, in Birmingham.... came over on one of the immigrant boats, and worked in the factories of Handsworth. But I couldn't take the life, especially the colour prejudice, especially since I was a Rastaman, full of the knowledge and pride of Marcus Garvey's philosophy. "

"One day I just packed up my savings, put a bag on my shoulder and hit the Channel Ferry. Next thing you know, I was in France and then Morocco (What a terrible place that is), and just started hitching rides on trucks, jeeps, buses until I reached to Addis. I have been here ever since."

We all digested this information, then Joseph asked: "How you manage without a woman out here?" We all laughed.
Isaac was serious though.

131

"Once, some sisters from the Sons of Jacob Organization came out here, and one of them took my fancy, and she decided to stay and live with me. We were alright for a while, and she even got pregnant for me. But when time came for her to give birth, she got a fever and there were complications and she needed the medical care that we could only get in Addis. So we asked the Sons of Jacob elder in Addis who holds their bank account, to pay for the hospital bill so we could take her in to have the baby, but the man said the money was only for the development of Shashemane, and he couldn't spend it on a private case.

"What happened?" I asked.

He hung his head, then shook it.
"We managed to save her life, but the baby died-- it was a boy, a son-- she just barely lived herself. As soon as she could travel, she took her return ticket, cut off her locks and went back to Jamaica. When I last heard, she was living in Miami and married to an insurance salesman..."

There was a long silence. "In a way," Isaac continued, "I am kinda glad I never locksed. I see so many Rasta locks and trim, and so many who are Rastafari and didn't locks, that I realize locks is not a necessary part of Rasta. Sometimes it is just vanity, or a disguise. For me, Rasta is deeds. A blind man must be able to know you are Rasta from the way you speak, the things you do, the love you bring to people's lives."

"I thought you were a Sons of Jacob," said Mikey, obviously hurt that the organization he was so proud of should be seen in a negative light.

"No, I think your mansion has a work to perform, to gather the congregation together according to their tribes. But for myself, I am Ethiopian Orthodox. We don't locks. We wear our hair like the Emperor, who worshipped in the Orthodox Faith."

Then Joseph said: "I go to the Orthodox Church in Kingston a few times, and it was really nice." Joseph smiled. "Many mansions in Rastafari, and all of them sweet."

Joseph certainly knew how to prevent a war, which from the look on Mikey's face was about to break out on the subject of the Church and the Tribes.

It was lovely to be at Shashemane, but after a few days, the realities of how hard life there was, made us all a little depressed. For a start, we had very little food and what we had brought soon finished, as we shared what we had with everyone there. So Joseph sent some of his US Dollars Travellers Cheques into Addis, and in two day's the two brothers who went returned with supplies and word that the other parcels which had left behind at Customs, still could not be cleared due to the kind of red tape which always faced Rasta entering Ethiopia.

As you can imagine, Joseph was angry that with all his money he had not been able to help change the situation, and this depressed him further. He felt as powerless as he had when he was penniless in the ghetto.

What really depressed me, was the presence of Sam, the journalist. You notice, I didn't even tell you he was among our special 'family'. To me, he was like when you take a booga out of your nose and can't get off of your finger....that was how I felt about him. I know it's not Christlike to feel so, but I'm telling you like it was. After the suggestion he put to me the last time we met, I was glad that he could see Peter and see the kind of man I could be interested in.

But when he and Peter met, he just shook Peter's hand and said with a smile, "Glad to meet you. Your wife thinks I'm a CIA spy!" and laughed.

"Are you?" Peter asked, noticing my grim expression.

Sam laughed. "I'm what you call a groupie. I love the music, the movement, the man. In the beginning, I was just out for the best story, the top news-- and nowadays Joseph is always top news. But now, it's more than that. It's a story, and I want to follow it to the ending."
He opened his arms wide and looked at Peter.

Peter turned to me. "That sounds like a perfectly true answer," he said.

"Now Ashanti," he said gently, and with a smile, "It is because he is WHITE that you don't like him?"

I was so shocked that I couldn't answer him. My mind raced with all kinds of self questions, but when THAT question came around again, I had to admit to myself that that was a big part of my feelings against Sam.

"A dat me feel too," said Joseph with a sly smile.

"But Ashanti," Peter smiled again gently, "you can't hate anyone for their colour, because you would just be as bad as those who hate you for your colour."

"But I didn't enslave them, and brutalize them, and pauperize them." I shot it out, I couldn't help it.

"No sis. Love must be the only emotion. That is how to conquer hate." Peter responded. "Look at Selassie after the Italians were defeated. He told the Ethiopians they should forgive their enemies so that they could put productive energy into rebuilding their country."

A voice behind me said: "It was Je-sus Christ who taught Selassie that principle, when he said we should love our enemies and forgive those who have wrongfully used us." It was the Shashemane brother, Isaac, who had said he was a member of the Orthodox Church.

Bringing the name 'Christ' into a Rasta reasoning, was always cause for a pause....

But the conversation returned to the subject, namely the teaching I was receiving.

"But what about Joseph's songs?" I asked. "They make us hate the white man."

"No sis. No. Please never say that." Joseph was quick.

"What I songs make you hate, is the evil ways of Babylon, hate the Satan ways that you have learned from Babylon, and to hate to be far from Zion. I kill society with I songs, not with violence, but I show man-and-man say I can understand wha' make dem deal with violence."

"You know, Sister," it was Red Dread. "This 'hate white' problem was one I had to deal with close up, because I mother is white, and in fact she had to live down a lot of scorn, and being spat upon in the street, just because she loved a Black man and let him love her. And when he left her, because he couldn't take the pressure, it was she who brought me up and was the only person between the whites who hated me because I was black and the blacks who hated me because I was half-white."

"I situation was kinda different," Joseph came in. "I curse the white man who took my mother but wouldn't marry her and accept his child—me. It's those kind of ways of the white man towards black, that cause I to see how man is wicked to man and how white ruled man so long, that white power doesn't need any morals anymore-- whatever they do is law. White morals caused slavery and apartheid, so I sing to show white morality that I see its sins, and I shout them out for I Black bothers and sisters to take notice.

"But all the time I am saying 'come out of Babylon', I message is for white man too, because he is I brother from JAH and he has as much chance of salvation as I, so I message is for Iniversal Inity and Love."

"You really mean that?" Sam asked in amazement. "I never understood that from your songs."

"Well, whole heap of white man, chiney man, coolie man, AND black man see that message in my songs. That is why we have so much white Rasta, chiney Rasta and coolie Rasta."

Sam just scratched his bald spot. "I guess that's what we whites see in your lyrics that make us want to stand up with you. It's not just that we feel for the cause of the poor and exploited. We do. But the real reason is that we also hope for salvation through doing right-- just like all of God's children. In the sixties Dylan was the messenger, in the seventies it is you Joseph."

"And why not the Eighties and Nineties too?", Joseph grinned, and we all laughed and the tension was broken.

Sam came over to me with his arms opened. "Sister Shanty, is jus' a love," he said with trying-Jamaican accent, and we all laughed again, as he hugged me.

We were friends of sorts after that. I still feel a way about the money he and the others like him have made out of Joseph's story, but JAH has his reasons, so let me just write my story for the record, and place it in the good company of the stories Sam and others like him have written about the remarkable man who was Joseph.

*   *   *   *

After a week at Shashemane, we felt like we were at a dead end, not at all like pioneers on the edge of a new world. The settlers there were brave survivors, each fiercely defending their territory and rights, but it was not the place we dreamed we could rest and be at peace in. Even communication with the native Ethiopians was difficult, as the settlers had mastered few words of Amharic. How true was Garvey's instruction that we should prepare our minds and skills for the journey home. How true was Selassie I's advice that we send first our highest and most skilled persons to establish our new home.

Joseph expressed his boredom by being unable to sing at all. The fountain of music that usually poured out of him, was dried up. He even forbade us to play his music on the cassette tape recorder.

In the cool of one evening, the Orthodox brother, Isaac, put on a tape recording he had made of a church service, as part of his meditations.

We couldn't understand the words, but the chanted music of the liturgy, the sounds of bells tinkling and bells being rung, as well as the responses of the congregation, it reminded Peter of something inside him.

"Let's go up to Lallibella," he announced in the silence.

"What's that?" Sam asked.

"It's a place where one of the first Ethiopian Kings built a lot of churches from the stone mountains. He and his followers chipped down one whole mountain in the shape of a church, and when they got down deep enough, they made doors and windows, and then they chipped their way inside and made rooms and seats, and an altar. And then they painted the insides with some beautiful visions of JAH Father and his saints." Peter explained.

"It's a place I've heard about and a place I want to see. I don't really believe it exists, to tell you the truth. But something inside me makes me want to be there, even more than here in Shashemane. I feel there is a message there for me."

Joseph was naturally interested in the 'mystic' of it.... "A message for Peter. Yes, let's go to Lalibela and look for Peter's message."

"Lallibella?" Red Dread rubbed his chin. "I've heard of it. Yes it's suppose to be real."

"It certainly is real," said Brother Isaac. "Unchanged since its creation four centuries ago. The whole city is made of churches, with tunnels connecting them with one another, all cut from the living rock. It is about two and half days journey from here, and the pilgrims often make their journey to the holy city. Some of the churches have a special dedication which prevents anyone except priests to enter, and some forbid the entry of women. But there are many beautiful things to be seen at Lallibella, especially the paintings on the wall and ceilings of churches."

"I have been there once, and the beauty is wonderful to behold. If you really want to go, I can guide you to a spot where someone who knows the way can be found."

Sam sputtered. "That must be quite a tough trip. Should we venture so far away from Addis Ababa?" He looked protectively around at his cameras, tape recorders, notebooks and you could see he was only thinking of his expensive equipment and the burden of carrying it all.

Red Dread made the decision for us all.
"Come on. An adventure would be much better than just sitting around here. We may never get to Ethiopia again."

Brother Isaac was pleased.
"Come let us prepare. We must carry food and camping equipment." He turned to Joseph with a smile. "I knew your visit here was for a divine reason. I've been waiting to return to Lallibella."

We sent into Addis for supplies and also to rent a vehicle. What eventually arrived two days later was a very old VW bus, but Peter and Joseph checked under the engine cover, and after a hour or two came up declaring that it was road worthy. So we packed our gear and ourselves into the vehicle and set off, chanting Psalms 87, 91, and especially Psalm 121 for strength, guidance and protection for our journey.

And what an amazing journey it was. Red Dread insisted on flying a Red, Gold and Green flag out the window of our vehicle. Inside were Joseph, Peter and I, Sam, Brother Isaac and Mikey. We had bedrolls, a stove, blanket, food and a special bag of Shashemane herb, grown by the settlers in violation of Ethiopian law, but welcomed for the meditations of I and I Rastafari.

Driving through Ethiopia was the most wonderful and at the same time the strangest experience I have ever had. Looking back at it, being able to see it like a fly on the wall, I can see how strange we must have seemed as we drove through.

When Sam was driving, with Brother Isaac in front guiding him, no one paid much attention to us, accustomed to seeing a white man with an Ethiopian guide, it seemed. But when Red Dread took the wheel with Joseph or Peter map-reading, all locks flying, our passage was slowed by the people's attention. When we passed through villages and they saw the dreads and realized we were strangers, our reception was as if we come from a new planet, strange gods, perhaps.

The countryside was very African, but it was the Ethiopian people who made it look interesting. They were such good looking Black people. Their eyes were round and their noses were regal in shape and size. Their mouths were deep red brown, and full. Everyone stood and sat erect, proud like statues, even the elders.

What made the scenery pretty was that most people wore the white shama dress-- a length of cotton cloth with embroidered edges, draped over the body like a cloak. The women used it to cover their heads or to make a private screen behind which to breast feed children, pray, or simply escape the eyes of strangers. Under the shama, they wore long white skirts, while the men wore trousers of the same cloth and draped the shamas around their shoulders like Roman togas.

We saw many small houses, eight sided or round like the churches which were everywhere. In fact, it was usually only in the church yards one would see trees, as most others had been cut down for firewood. This was one of the reasons for the famine, but we didn't pass through the real famine areas, though we could see the poverty of the peasant people.

At the same time we were observing reality, we in the bus were of course seeing it as the country of JAH, and of Selassie I, where he had ruled and lived, and fought the Italians, where he was crowned King, and where, because of H.I.M we sons and daughters of Africa abroad could hope to return to Africa to live.

This was also of course the country, the country that had rejected the King, where a new set of un-royal masters ruled, masters who said they had killed the King, but could not show us a grave....

Yes, it was quite a strange journey, full of feelings of the present, the past and the imaginary future. And it was certainly Joseph's journey as much as Peter's for even though it had been Peter's suggestion that we go to Lallibella, without Joseph-- without his money and what he stood for-- we would not have been where we were. We also knew that being in Ethiopia was the most important event in Joseph's life so far, and he wanted it to be an event of significance.

We stopped the first two nights in the largest town we could find by evening. With a language dictionary, the few words Brother Isaac knew, and by pointing to the Ethiopian crosses we wore, we were directed to a church each time. On the second evening, the Priest who welcomed us showed us to sleeping accommodation which we could see had been given up by the priests themselves. Then he invited us to join the faithful in prayer, which seemed to be continuous throughout the night and day.

We refreshed ourselves and entered the small church, and as we came in each of us spent a few moments in silent meditation, before taking a seat. You don't have to be specially religious to feel a sense of peace and holiness when entering a church....a feeling of wanting to alone with one's personal god in a place of spirituality.

We sat there, stood sometimes, sometimes knelt as the congregation did. We couldn't understand the chants, but we were gripped by beauty of the sounds and the obedience of the people, their humbleness.

A priest came down the aisle with a burner of incense, followed by a young boy, bearing a large silver cross, and the priest swung the incense burner towards us where we sat at the back of the small church and the youth made obeisance with the cross towards us, and the odor of the incense covered us all with its holy smell.

The cloud of incense so united us, that we all got up as if at one sign and went outside. Joseph led the way to a tree, on whose large roots he sat, and we stood and sat around, facing the last glows of the sun in a red and purple sky over a green-brown land.

"That's what I liked about the church in Kingston." Joseph broke our silence. "It was the first church that I ever felt was holy."

"What do you mean by that?" asked Mikey, warningly. Joseph looked him in the eye.

"Like that church was RIGHT."

Mikey exploded into anger.

"Me no like no bloodclaat church. Church is just a fuckery to fuck up man brain, make man dependent on another man to save his soul. Church is responsible for more sodomy, more prostitution, more divorce, more lesbian, more rape, more murder, than any other institution on earth; you hear me?"

He was shouting, his eyes wide.

"Church is for battymen and old women.
This living flesh is my temple, and if it is my temple, then my priest is inside it.
Therefore, I am my own church and my own priest.
Don't talk to me about n blood-claat church."

"But to join an organization, and to give up your power to make decisions over to one man, or a few men, is just the same as joining a church," said Red Dread.
"No matter how much you hate the institution of 'church' you have to see that most of the other mansions of Rastafari are just one kind of church or another, praising His Majesty and the Father JAH." This was from Red Dread.

"How can you hate the Orthodox Church so much?"

"Who say me hate Orthodox Church?" Mikey was even more angry.

"Me hate EVERY bloodclaat church... Look at how them suck us in, blow incense over us and hypnotize us in them obeah mumbo jumbo."

Peter spoke trying to calm the situation....

"Well, I wouldn't call it obeah, but seeing the effect church has on people, I can truly understand the socialist philosophy which says that religion is like a drug that people get addicted to. But at the same time because I am Rastafari, I have to acknowledge that the human animal feels joy in expressing unity with its creator, and human animals like to congregate together to express this recognition of union. This is why I&I chant Nyabingi, for the coming together of voices and souls in praise of JAH. So Nyabingi is as much church as this church. Nyabingi is the Old Testament of JAH; Church is the New Testament of the Ethiopian Black Christ."

"Me no check for NYABINGI, neither," Mikey spat out. "Too much praises and too little action. Too many old man trying to hold on to the past. Any man who block pen and paper and education, can't lead I to Zion."

Red Dread entered the reasoning. "If the elders had not held on to the old ways, there would not have been anything for us youngsters to inherit and shape, as the new breed of Rastas are doing now....changing the movement gradually to cope with world changes, so that the city we build will be modern, even while it still maintains its old values and traditions."

"But I must say that as a member of the Ethiopian World Federation, I respect and admire how the Sons of Jacob has organized its membership in a disciplined way, and also recruited some top brains among the young Rastas. We in EWF in England are trying to organize along similar lines, but the only difference with us is that we are split up in different chapters which, even though we share a common constitution, we don't share a common I-nity. I think I-nity is the best example Sons of Jacob has to show I&I."

Mikey had no comment to make, but seemed satisfied with the praise of his 'mansion'.

"For JAH sake, stop quarreling about Church and mansions and all the things that divide Rasta," Joseph spread his hands between us.

"Every part of Rasta has a purpose, to bring knowledge."
Joseph spoke strong.
"Some part tell I of I Tribe; some of I Story. Some chant I hymns, some are the Church in which I&I praise Christ, the Man who I&I say is reborn in Selassie I. For if we say Selassie I is Christ reborn, then we must chant and praise Christ also, who was before Selassie. There MUST be a place for that, if there is a place for all else that is divine in this Earths Creation. And I&I must not be prejudiced or too proud to bow to CHRIST. HE is who WE see in Selassie I, and Selassie I we see the Father, because the Son came from the Father, and the Father was in the Son."

He was quite excited, bobbing up and down with energy on the big root he was resting on. His locks flopped around his frowning face and active mouth, and we were all fixed on his words.

"Sometimes I wish that all I can be remembered for is to be like the wick of a candle. Ever standing upright in the middle of the hottest fire, burning yet not being burnt, surrounded by hotter fire, but the hottest fire is the outer shield of fire, the protecting flame of JAH.'

Joseph got to his feet now, and he was speaking to himself, as much as to us. "The wax supporting me may eventually run out, and I will disappear, but all I want people to say is that while I was there, I shed some Light. That's all, I-a. Let there be Peace, for then there will be Light."

Joseph told me-- on his sickbed, up at the mountain monastery of Debre Zeit where he chose to rest among the priests, when he knew doctors could do nothing more for his flesh temple -- that what happened next was the most surprising (he said 'thunderous') thing that ever happened in his life. He said it was the single event that made him realize the purpose of life, the experience that gave the energy for the revolution he released on the world on his return from Ethiopia.

A man suddenly appeared, literally appeared, standing beside our group. He held up his hand to Joseph in a gesture of greeting and said:
"Well done. You have now entered the First Circle. Are you ready for your journey?"

We had been looking at Joseph as he spoke, and did not see the man walk up to us, so his voice and words startled us, as you can imagine. But to his dying day, Joseph swore the man simply appeared as if by magic.

Joseph was surprised, but when he heard the man's question, he did a strange thing. He laughed, threw back his head and laughed. And of course, our tensions left us.

"Oh, you are the guide. I didn't see you come," Joseph spoke to the man, and we joined Joseph in assuming he was the guide to Lallibella whom Isaac had promised to find. We were supposed to wait this night at his church for the guide, then set off in the morning.

He was an olive-skinned Ethiopian, wearing a shama wrapped around him which exposed brown, muscled calves and sandalled feet. His hair was combed upward like a crown, priest-style, and he had the small wispy beard of a young man perhaps in his 20's. In his hand carried a tall walking stick.

"We will leave now and sleep on the road," were his next words. We were surprised at his change of plans, and tried to get an explanation, but our guide ignored us.

"Now," he commanded softly. Joseph rested his head sideways on his chin, thinking, for a while. We waited.

"Yes, I'm ready," he finally said.

Our guide then bent over and whispered something into Joseph's ear which none of us could hear, but which made him jump back. Then he settled down and put his arms as if they were birds wings, and then looked our guide deep in the eyes.

"Come. Let's go."

CHAPTER NINE

"Because he hath set his love upon me, therefore will I deliver him: I will set him on high, because he hath known my name. (JAHOVAH-I-ADONAI). PSALM 87; Vs. 1-2

We walked towards the dusk, our caravan of eight souls and two donkeys laden with our things and food. As night drew on, we camped with our backs against a giant tree trunk, built a fire, and couldn't sleep all night for the howling and roars of the lions and hyenas in the darkness. All of us were frightened, but couldn't show how much.

But our guide just sat by the lantern, he had brought and read from a book which must have been his liturgy, for sometimes he moved his lips.

By morning we had drunk some strong bittersweet Ethiopian coffee, eaten a hard small loaf of bread and a piece of goat's cheese, and we all set off again.

The road was strange. A track really. Not the road we expected, though we knew Lallibella was not much changed since the days of King Lallibella who caused this religious wonder of the world to be created. Lallibella was where Ethiopian man, through Kings and Priests celebrated Christ and God in his highest, holiest form, making their tribute the painstaking work of stonecutting, each chip sacred to the glory of JAH and His Saints. Yes, we knew the road would be old, but surely it would be more used, more travelled. We seemed to be the only ones on it.

By about ten in the morning, a kind of hazy light began to cover us, seeming to come from low clouds in the rocky river bankside track we were taking. Soon the track grew narrower and steeper, so that our Guide stopped us and walked back to the donkeys from whose packs he extracted some walking sticks similar to the one he was using to balance himself so expertly. Soon we too were depending on the support the stout sticks gave us from falling on the tricky ground.

There were, of course, the usual run of comments, groans, stumbles, laughs, fears, expressed by all of us on this trip, but Joseph alone was silent the whole way. He walked behind the guide (whose name he said was Mikael) putting his feet where his had been. When he slipped, he looked to no one to help him, even though we knew that sometimes his right lung gave him some pain where the gunshot had broken the rib over it. He just picked himself up and went on, not seeming to hear us.

I wondered what it was that the guide had said to him that had such a power on him, and I asked him when we stopped for lunch of bread and cheese with thick honey still in the comb brought up by Mikael from a calabash.

"What did he say to you?" I asked. "It's not time to tell you yet," was his reply, and I turned back to eating.

The hazy light made everything seem unreal. You couldn't say what time it was, whether 12 or 3 or 5 o'cclock. We just knew that we had been walking a long way. We couldn't see the sun, only this hazy light and the red brown earth, with here and there some green trees. Strange landscape. Very unusual. I know I'd recognize it if I ever saw it again.

Sam took some pictures with one of his many cameras, and said that the light made the film act like a yellow filter, so he had to adjust his exposures.

Red Dread, whose sturdy, golden Amazon body seemed made expressly for this journey, was more preoccupied with his physical expenditure, than to worry about the end result of this strange journey. "I knew something like this was going to happen. If all seven Idren like I&I are together in a place like Ethiopia, something of the cosmic mus' enfold us. Vibration of so many upfull Idren must be strong. Electricity....." was his comment.

About ten minutes after we set off again, a rainbow started to follow us. Truly. A rainbow started to follow over our heads.

JOSEPH - A RASTA REGGAE FABLE

We could see its beginning on a red hillside far on our left, and see its end in the low grass that fringed the right edge of the valley we trod. At first we pointed it out with pleasant surprise and joy, but when it stayed and stayed over our heads for a long time we realized it was walking with us. It made us feel truly strange for the first time, a little frightened.

And then we felt suddenly strong and-- well, holy. Like the rainbow was a blessing from JAH. So we just walked with it. In silence. Peter held my hand. I was so glad he did.

"This is not the road to Lallibella," Joseph announced what we had all guessed by now. We did not dare ask where we were going, nor who our guide really was. But we were soon rewarded with knowledge.

Over another of the endless hills we suddenly saw a round valley deep below us. It was bright green, with trees and, on closer look, food being cultivated and flowering vines and flowers. As we started descending towards its center, the rainbow stopped over us.

What we thought were large white limestone rocks lying in the valley, turned out, as we drew closer to be domed buildings, each with a hole in the top, and small entrances and windows, all carefully constructed to look like large stones from afar. It didn't take long to reach a level spot in the central floor of the valley, down a well-used track between rows of fruit trees and vegetables growing in the shades. Across on one side, we could see and hear the ripple and gurgle of a spring of water from a rock.

Our guide Mikael gave a sound, and several men in white priest robes came out of the domed houses and made the benediction of Peace and Love with him-- three bows over the shoulders of beloved brethren-- and then greeted us the same. Some offered us small stones to rest on, and helped us off with our backpacks.

And then they did a wonderful thing.

148

Seven of them, one for each of us, knelt down, removed our shoes and sandals, and washed our feet with water in silver bowls.

That simple but wonderful act humbled us totally. We knew we were in the presence of great goodness. We looked at each other silently. Joseph just looked out in the distance.

We were taken each to a dwelling in the round domes. Each, we discovered when we talked about it later, was a Temple to a Saint of the Ethiopian Church.

Mine was a shrine to the Virgin Mary. Inside the dome, the ceiling was deep blue with white and silver stars and a golden moon. Through a small opening in the roof, light shone at various times in the day on several paintings and icons of the Blessed Mother and Her Child.

My bed of thick mats on the floor, was covered in deep blue velvet, edged with gold, and lots of soft pillows in royal silks. Beside the top of the bed was a small table inlaid with ivory, on which was a small saucer of holy oil and a candle, which I lit and made the sign of Christ over the four corners of my flesh temple.

There was a large red velvet cushion in the middle of which an illustrated version in full colour of the Kebra Negast-- the Ethiopian Book of the Kings which contains Ethiopia religious and national history from the days of Solomon and Queen Makeda of Sheba. I lay down and leafed through the pages, looking at the beautiful illustrations of this amazing story.

Looking at the story and the pictures of Black people, King Solomon and his courtiers, Queen Makeda and her caravan, it reminded me that it was when I heard that the Queen of Sheba was a black woman, way back around one of my father's Wareika campfires, that I decided that identifying with Rastafari was a good thing to do. I remember being glad to learn of one great black person in the Bible, later followed by the equally important realization that if the Bible story was set in Africa, then its characters must have been African people.

Including Christ.

Now here, in this pictorial Ethiopian history, I was seeing with my eyes the racial lineage from Solomon and David through Christ which was part of the Ethiopian history. At the same time I was being reminded of my father, and of my own beginnings. What a co-incidental book to find in such a place, I marvelled.

When I lay down on the bed, on the ceiling in front of my eyes I could see a portrait of the Black Madonna and Child, so that all the times my contemplation was fixed on this woman-- like myself, a female-- It was automatic that I sent up my prayers to JAH through Her, the Mother I hoped I would one day be, with Peter the Father. That had so far escaped us.

After I slept restfully from the long walk, I woke and seeing it was still light, I freshed in a large pail of water set behind a curtain in the dwelling, and changed into a long white robe that was put there for my use. While I slept, food had been placed on a table by the door, and I ate meat in sauce with grain like cornmeal, rice, and juicy green pods like a cross between okra and a pepper. There was cheese, honey and thick crisp biscuits on a plate, coffee and peeled oranges. To end the feast, there was a sweet like an almond candy.

I needed company, so I came outside to find the brothers in conversation, seated on benches under a tree.

"Where are we really?" Sam was asking.
"Wherever we are, what an amazing place to be!" Peter answered.

"Where's Joseph?" I asked.

"That's what were just wondering," Peter turned to welcome me.

"I believe that these priests heard that the great Joseph Planter was in Ethiopia and wanted their monastery to get some publicity, so they hijacked us here."

We laughed, long. "But," he continued, "How would we explain the rainbow?" We laughed again, but not so long.

Red Dread went into his neckbag for his herb and began to make a spliff. But one of the priests materialized with a tray bearing clay cutchies-- even a woman's pipe-- and sticky, green brown buds of sensimilla, and even a firestick.

That was another shock. Who were these priests?
They hardly spoke English, but our guide Mikel was quite at home with them.

Our only concern was Joseph.

"He's still in his temple," said Red Dread. "There's a priest sitting at the door."

He turned to us.
"My temple is to the Archangel Mikael. I didn't know there was such a saint. It's the nicest place I've ever been in. I've never been in a temple to a Black saint before."

"Me neither," said Peter. "Mine is of the Archangel Gabriel."
"Who was he?" I asked.
"Who IS he," Peter corrected. "He is the angel Ethiopian women pray to for a child."

"Women and men, also," said the priest who sat with us. "Man and woman journey, some of them on their knees, miles up the road to the Cathedral of St. Gabriel each year, to pray for a child, or to thank St. Gabriel for the gift of one."

He walked over to me, took my hand and led me over to Peter. "You and he have some prayers to say in that temple. On your last night here, you will be allowed."

At first I felt astonished at how this man was interfering in my business-- wondering how he even knew-- but there was no rude reference in what he said. He stated it simply as fact, and I had to withdraw my anger.

"Why aren't we in Lallibella?" the priest asked. "To see the wonders of man's hand in praise to JAH? Here we are of JAH himself."

JAH! The word whispered on his lips like a soft wave breaking on the shore.

"JAH," he said.

"You called Him JAH," Mikey said at last.

"Yes. That is one of the names of HIM, and it is a powerful name. We know that you know that name, and use it. That is why we brought you here. Now you must eat and rest and be filled with knowledge you will need for your return to the world outside this place. You have a work to do, especially for Joseph."

Somewhere under the trees, a priest started playing on a round-bellied instrument with strings. Bells joined him in rhythm and a chant started among the priests not far away. It was a divine chanting, and it had a rhythm, so Red Dread made a drum out of the bench in front of him, and Mikey turned his gourd into one too, and Ethiopia and Jamaica met in oneness in praise to our Father JAH and Brother Christ-us I Selassie I, Rastafari--human flesh that had caused us to see the Creator and had brought us to this place.

The chant made a melody that made me want to find the harmony with my voice, and I did, lending the only instrument I had, to the divine choir. Our music and rhythms grew bolder, stronger, louder, happier, climaxed. Even Sam was a smiling part of our joy and ardor, our utter ecstasy at feeling the God-spirit within us fill every part of our souls, brain and consciousness.

"We go take communion now." Our host bid us goodnight in the dusk that was gathering as our song ended. And they went off to a distant part of the valley, from where we could hear their chants and prayer faintly throughout the night.

Under bright stars, we listened to the sounds of worship, and the night insects. It seemed as if there was so much we should speak about, so much that was obviously going around in everyone's minds. But somehow, what we were thinking seemed to be communicated around our minds, without us even having to utter the sounds. I felt as if I was hearing a great conversation of people, all talking and thinking about great positive ideas and philosophical truths, all pouring forth from a fountain of loving unity of minds and souls. I felt a oneness that made me understand how identical twins felt, or a child bonded to its mother.

And then an echo of "Hallelujah" from the far away temple, the chord broke into our separate souls.

"I'm tired." said Red Dread.
"I'm looking forward to sleeping in my bed," said Mikey.

"I think I'll stay and look at the stars," Sam said flatly. We all wanted to ask him who was the Saint with whom he slept, but wanted him to tell us of his own free will. He didn't, so we went to our domes, leaving him alone.

CHAPTER TEN

*"And I saw the seven angels which stood before God (JAH);
And another angel came and stood at the altar, having a
golden censer; and there was given unto him much incense,
that he should offer it with the prayers of all saints upon the
golden altar which was before the throne. And the smoke of the
incense which came with the prayers of the saints ascended up
before God (JAH) out of the angel's hand."*
REVELATION 8: VS. 2, 3, 4.

The next morning, after breakfast, the priest brought out great
boxes which he opened, showing us hundreds of books and
scrolls painted with beautiful colours and pictures, edged with
real gold. None were in English, so we could only look, but we
could see they were very valuable and old, and holy.

What was great about them, was that all people painted in the
holy pictures were Black. And beautiful. They were all so regal
and grand and well-dressed and bright-eyed.

"Church propaganda," snorted Mikey. "I'm going for a walk."
And off he marched.

 priest followed him.
"I want to be alone," Mikey protested.
The priest smiled patiently.
"You cannot be. Come and let me show you where we grow the
collie herb."

Mikey couldn't help laughing.
"Come on, then."

Sam was busy taking pictures, peering into his equipment,
cleaning it, quiet. Peter was sitting, listening to a priest tell him
a story of the Ethiopian Church, how it was founded during the
time of the Apostles, and how Ethiopia had been a Christian
Kingdom ever since. He told the great Kings of Ethiopia, who
were great because they made the Church the centre of the
Kingdom.

They told of the Martyrs, like King Theodoros, who committed suicide at the Battle of Magdala, rather than fall into the hands of the English soldiers who were plundering the city of its wealth and holy treasures. He told of Lij Tafari, the man who became Emperor Haile Selassie, the First, who helped dethrone a King who wanted to change Ethiopia from worshipping Christ, to serve Allah instead.

He told them of the seven sacraments of the Church, and read them part of the Anaphora of St. John the Divine. He explained things simply and interestingly. Peter was very thoughtful when he was finished.

We ate a lunch of salad made out of about 20 different vegetables, some of which I had never eaten before. After that, some sweet yogurt made from goat's milk.

And still Joseph had not come to join us.
Nor did he come at dinner time.
The same priest still sat outside his door.

That night as I went to bed, I saw on my pillow a gold box. When I opened it, I saw it contained pages of a document in English.

"THE PRAYER OF THE VIRGIN MARY", I read.

"One of the holiest prayers of the Ethiopian Church." was written on the second leaf of its document, but I soon realized it was in truth not just a book, but a prayer to be prayed out loud, so I started again, reading out loud this time.

The Prayer of the Virgin Mary is a long, passionate plea from the Mother, Mary, to her Son, to assist in saving the life of St. John. The prayer is so earnest, that Christ answers his Mother. She promises that the words of the prayer are so powerful, that anyone who prays the prayer, using the holy names of God contained in it, and anointing oneself with holy oil, will receive any favor or blessing asked for.

I was amazed that such a prayer existed. Did it work? Even if it didn't, there could be no harm in spending an hour or so reading such wonderful words out loud.

I fell asleep with my arms around the box. I could hardly wait till morning to speak to Peter. As soon as I could, I dressed and went out to the clearing under the trees where he sat.

"They gave me a prayer last night. The Prayer of...."

"...The Virgin Mary." Peter finished my sentence. How incredible."

The same thought occurred to us at the same time.
"Let's pray it tonight, together. If we can." I begged him.

"Ashanti...I have been thinking a lot. Don't laugh." He paused. "I want to be baptized. Here. In the Ethiopian Church. I want to set my soul right with JAH and I realized that this corny thing called 'baptism' is really the only door we can travel through to eternity. I want to be baptized."

"Why?" I asked him. It seemed such an un-Rasta thing to do.

"Boy, sis. I just feel it's right. It's like, I was reading my Book last night and I came to the part where Jesus Christ met John the Baptist, and how he asked John to baptize Him. Well, I meditated on it a while. You know how all these Church people always check for baptism to wash away your sins to wash, like a big load of washing."

We both laughed.

"But when I read it last night I thought how Christ didn't have any sins, and still he wanted to be baptized. So I asked myself why, and then the Book turned itself to where Christ said that the only way we can see Zion is if we look into ourselves as sinners and seek cleansing, with faith. Faith, that if we do that, the Holy Father will give a new life-- an everliving life, clean and fresh, like the new name he promised us.

"Well, I thought about it a long time. I don't have no sins. That's what I said. But when I check it out, I have a whole heap of sins. Anger -- I have a lot of anger all the time. And pride. That is what make me get into a lot of war with man-and-man. You see, sin is not just murder and adultery, and them thing. Sin is anything that is not like Christ." I had to agree with him.

"We have to be good, equal at all times, pure, like Selassie. Is like that I must be pure, without sins.

"Then what-- you 'fraid to die?" I asked him.

"No. Me no 'fraid to dead. Me know say dead is just a door to Zion. But me 'fraid to dead without the key to the door, and I feel say to baptize is to hold the key."

What he said made me think. It made sense, when I thought about it. I never thought about baptism before. Now I realized that all the time I was thinking just because I was living a righteous Rasta life, I was certain of my place in Zion, that I was not really qualified.

All of a sudden, I wanted to be baptized too.

Peter spoke into the far-away place my mind had gone.
"You see what I mean?"

"Yes. I see."
He got up and went over to one of the priests who were never far away, and when he came back he said:
""It's alright. We goin' baptize today."

*   *   *   *

They came for us at about four in the afternoon. They brought two plain white robes for us, and we put them on over our clothes.
Then the priest, Mikael came.

"Come."

He led us through a path between domes, and we found ourselves walking through the garden towards the sound of the stream. The water was flowing out of a rock, pouring down in waterfall, to one stream. There were smooth stones, beside a deep pool of the stream, and we sat on them.

Then two other priests came, dressed in robes, carrying a large gold cross in front of them. The cross was the most beautiful Ethiopian cross I had ever seen, with jewels, pearls, diamonds, forming the points, corners and filigreed patterns of its beauty.

Then the priest signaled us to stand up, and put a small Bible in each of our hands. They started their Amharic chants then, waving a silver incense holder from a gold chain. The incense smelled like roses and frankincense mixed.

Mikael came up to us and took our hands, and led us into the water where another priest was standing. The water was icy cold, and I jumped to feel it. I wondered if I would catch a cold from the cold water, but before I could think of it again, my mind was filled with the fullness of what I was going to do. I felt a great oneness with Christ and his baptism. I trembled and tears came to my eyes, tears of emotion, pity for myself.

I found there was a prayer on my mind. "Father JAH, make me worthy to receive your Blessing. Make me worthy. Make me Yours."

The priest took Peter's head in his hands and bent it backwards gently into the water three times. I looked at Peter's face. His eyes were closed and his lips were moving. When the three times were done, the priest turned to me and did the same thing.

I held my breath, and the water rushed over me, icing my head through the thick mat of locks. Once. Twice. Three times.

"Holy Father, make me worthy to receive your Blessing." My mind repeated the prayer three times.

The chanting continued, and grew louder as we came out of the water. They led us up the bank to a tree and covered us in thick clothes from head to toe, then we sat down. The Bibles in our hands were wet but we still held them.

Then-- wonder of wonders-- a most amazing sight appeared. A line of old priests appeared on the path. They were the oldest men I have ever seen, really ancient, but quiet and walking strong. Their robes were shining in red, blue, green and gold trimmings. Their crosses on their chests were all gold and very large, some with precious stones on them. On their heads they wore crowns with crosses on them.

And in the centre of the procession they carried a stretcher on which rested Joseph.

"Rastafari!" Peter's voice was soft, but shocked. "Look how him mawga-- like him sick, goin' dead! How him get so sick since we get here?"

The priests made a circle in the water, and carried Joseph, still on the stretcher, into the pool. He raised himself up on one arm, looking pale and thin, his eyes not seeing anything. The cloud of incense was as thick as the smoke of a wood fire, and in the thick of it, they baptized Joseph.

As his head came up the third time, the smoke lifted up like someone had sucked it up, then Joseph threw back his head, heavy with its locks and yelled with a voice as strong as the Joseph we knew.

JAH! RASTAFARI!

Then we knew why we had been brought here.

In a daze we put on dry robes and followed Mikael through the now-coming night, back to the domes which we knew were churches, in one of which Joseph had been praying for three days and three nights.

Little bells were ringing, and all the priests carried small bells of various sizes and sounds in their hands, which they shook and chimed. The sound of the bells were the only noise we heard all evening, and through the night.

They led us both to Peter's temple, which I had not seen before. Inside, it was red-- all red except the bed which was covered in white animal skin. In the centre of the bed was a large cushion covered in white linen, on which lay a gold box, on the cover of which was an enamel painting of the Virgin Mary and Her Child riding on a donkey escorted by servants and warriors.

We opened the box and inside was a hand-written note which read:

"Those who truly believe will receive."

Peter took out the book and began to read. We took turns reading out loud, and when we came to the secret and holy names of JAH in the prayer, we chanted them together. When we came to the place that instructed us to anoint ourselves with oil, we dipped our fingers in the oil in a bowl beneath the crucifix on the table, and made the sign of the cross on our foreheads. And when it told us to ask for what we wanted, we asked.

It took us two hours to read the Prayer of the Virgin Mary. Then Peter closed the Book, put it back in the box, folded his arms tightly around me. We lay together silently for a long time, before we made the sweetest love we had made in our lives.

Was it our imagination that at the moment of our simultaneous climax, the bells outside rang very, very loudly?

And then stopped.

*   *   *   *

We left the next morning. Red Dread, with his bronze locks thick about his shoulders, a white shama draped around him, and his walking staff, was transformed by his experience in the St. John temple.

Mikey with an amused smile, later explained that his temple had been of St. Thomas, who doubted.

Peter and I were closer than ever.

Sam was unduly quiet.

And Joseph was his old self again, bright and full of life, and fat as if he had eaten all night to make up for the days of fasting.

There was Mikael, standing with the priests, who were tinkling their bells again, smiling all over their faces, especially the old ones, chanting prayers, blessings and farewells for us.

"What is the name of this place?" Joseph asked Mikael.

"The name of the fountain is Emmanuel," were his last words.

CHAPTER ELEVEN

"Behold, the days come, saith the Lord (JAH), that I will raise unto David a righteous Branch, and a King shall reign and prosper, and shall execute judgement and justice in the earth. In his days Judah shall be saved, and Israel shall dwell safely: and this is his name whereby he shall be called, THE LORD OUR RIGHTEOUSNESS. JEREMIAH 23; Vs 5-6

We fled from the airport to our London hotel, followed by cars of reporters and photographers. Outside the hotel was the same sort of bedlam we thought we had left at the airport. Crowds of people restrained behind metal barricades were screaming abuse at Joseph, while behind other barricades, Joseph's fans shouted his praise.

"Nigger! Go back to Africa!"

"We don't need your kind here!"

"Leave our women alone! Stick to monkeys like yourself!"

"Joseph! We love you!"

"Joseph! Sing us a song!"

Can you imagine it? I was terrified. The looks on some of the angry white faces were murderous. What was it all about?

We found out in our hotel suite of rooms, where the Tropic PR waited, worried, nervous. They held out press clippings dated the week after we had left for Ethiopia.

Joseph took the thick bundles and dropped on the table, where the scattering exposed some headlines:

"REGGAE STAR'S DRUG ORGY."
"I WAS THERE, SAYS MODEL/RECEPTIONIST"
"PEACE (?) AND LOVE?" was the most awful.

According to the story, there had been a wild party in the suite at Brown's Hotel, where ganja as well as cocaine were used, and several women were sexually enjoyed against there will by the many men gathered. According to the story, most of the men were Rastafarians. According to the story, Joseph had been there.

"It must have been the night we heard we got our visa, and the receptionist girl called to tell us we were making too much noise," Mikey deduced. "But there weren't any girls there. And we never had no cocaine. And Joseph wasn't there."

"Hey, I remember." Joseph recalled. "I went for a walk... found myself lost.. had to take a taxi back. You guys were in the main room, and I just wanted to be alone with my thoughts, so I never even bothered to tell you that I had come back. I just used the key to my room door and went to sleep. Your noise never even keep me awake."He shook his head.

"A-how them people lie so? Wha' this woman a-want to tell such a lie pon me for, eeh sah? Me no even remember the girl. Now see them have photo of she and me. When them take this?"

He pointed to a picture of a smiling Joseph being embraced by a smiling white girl, skimpily dressed.

"Remember when we checked in, she asked if she could take a picture with you?" Mikey reminded Joseph.

Poor Joseph. Women of all kinds were always showing him affection and admiration. He had long ago stopped showing his disapproval of the way some of them presented their physical selves. We women around Joseph would simply frown when we saw the tight pants, the low-cut, bra-less blouses, the red lips and nails and the painted faces of the many women who sought a smile, an admiring glance from Joseph.

Poor Joseph.
This is what they were going to use to 'kill' him.

"You know," said Peter. "An old man I knew in prison once explained to me what 'obeah' was. He said, a lot of people think obeah is a kind of black magic using oils and mystical chants and all kinds of guzum, and that is how obeah people take a lot of money from simple people. But Obeah is to think up the worst lie you can tell about a person, a lie they just cannot deny, no matter how they try, a lie that sticks to you and send out bad vibes, which eventually kill you. THAT, he said, is obeah."

"It look like them obeah you, Joseph."

"It's no use me saying I was not there," said Joseph. Bwoy, how come such an awful thing happen to me-- just now. If it's obeah, like you say Peter, then me haffi find the antidote. JAH wouldn't let me go through the experience me jus' have, and leave me without a prayer."

He turned to Patrick, one of the Tropic people.
"Get us out of here; somewhere quiet."

Patrick thought for a moment.

"Busha has a country home near Windsor... real country. I know you can use it."

We sent some dreads ahead of us through the hotel lobby, with heads covered up like they were Joseph hiding from the cameras, and while the Press and the crowd were mobbing them, we went out the underground parking lot in a big van – a bit dirty and dented on the outside, bu very comfortably laid out outside with carpets, cushion, food, drink and a small colour TV.

England is really a beautiful country, and when you're in a place like Windsor, where the people are well-off and content, life can appear gentle and very charming. Since Windsor is where the Queen of England's castle is, all the countryside surrounding is very beautiful, with round hills, meadows, field and farms, and gardens full of blooming roses of the late summer days.

Bush's country house was an Elizabethan version of this other luxurious lifestyles, full of Tudor antiques, Persian carpets and a staff of fourteen servants, including a butler.

Joseph refused to sleep in an antique four-poster bed, demanding that the mattress be placed on the floor, and there, with a view of the English countryside spread out before him, we sat and meditated, reasoned and prepared for the inevitable confrontation.

"I won't let them slime up my trip to Shashemane with their lies," Joseph was firm. "Whatsoever I do, I must use our visit to Ethiopia to show that the higher mission we are on, does not give us the time for slackness. I have to show them that my mind deal with higher things.

"But at the same time, I know that this is a planned trap. This scandal is not the start of things. This story began from the Peace Concert, when I got shot... and even before that. Maybe it began when you and Peter came to see me, Ashanti... or even before that, when I was a humble Rastaman dared to sing I songs of Black freedom to the world outside Jamaica."
He shook his head.

"This trap was planned to stop me, just like the gunshot. I will never know who shot me, because I was not shot by a man, but by the system. But I can't let down the sons and daughters of Israel, I&I whose reputation is so dependent on my actions. This smear is on all Israel, not just on I."

We let him think for a while, then he suddenly clicked two fingers together and said:

"You know what I must do? I have to do a show."

"A SHOW!" We were astonished!

Joseph smile and held up his hand to stop our reactions.
"A very special 'show'. A big, big, show, me bredrin. To answer all the questions."

He turned to me.

"Sister Shanty, call Patrick and tell him to get Busha here. I need to talk to him right away. We have a lot of preparations to do."

Sam got up.

"I must get in touch with people, change my clothes, get back to normal for a while. I can be here in two days, okay?"

Yes, Sam was still with us, still clicking his cameras, getting 'his' story. He picked up his camera bags and started to the door.

Then he turned and added with sour smile: "You know, whenever I hear you guys calling yourselves "Israel," it makes me wonder what the Jews of Israel feel about your claim to their title. I must interview a Rabbi one of these days."
And he continued picking up to go.

"Sam," Joseph's voice stopped him, and he turned.

"You're a Jew. How do you feel about this destruction by media that we are suffering. It's mostly Jews who control the world media, isn't it?"

"That's a lie!"

It jumped out of Sam before he could stop it. The hatred, the rage, and death showed big and red in his eyes and face.

"And so what if it is? I'm sick of being around you racist Rastas, you hate Jews so much. So what if Jews own the world! They own it because they worked hard for it, and they sure as hell aren't gonna let any bunch of halfwits like you guys come along and use Jewish media, or Jewish publishing, or Jewish films, to take over the world and make it like you want it to be!"

Mikey drew in his breath to reply angrily, saying "We don't hate Jews....," but Joseph quickly silenced him, allowing Sam to continue.

A flash of thunder burst in the air outside, and suddenly the English rain began to fall. Sam was glad for the pause, not even sensing the significance of the thunderclap and the rain to the rest of us.

"You know, you really think too much of yourselves." He slung his bag over his shoulder and started to the door. "I'm sick of being part of this travelling circus. I'm sick of following you around like you're some damn prince, or saint or something. You're nothing but a little rass Jamaican boy who sang some songs in ganja smoke. Now, let's see you get out this jam."

With a gasp of breath, I rose up to speak, to spit on him, to strike the damn white man DOWN, KILL HIM.

But quickly Joseph put out his hand and dragged me sitting down again, swallowing my breath, words, actions.

"Careful, Sister Shanty...don't curse. Bless him. Bless him for showing us the truth of him. He has done what he had to do...what he was sent to do. Now his work is finally over."
He looked straight into Sam's eyes as he spoke.

Peter sprang to his feet, blocking the door.
"Him cyan' go until him tell me who-fa Temple the priest-dem put him in at Emmanuel!"

He looked as if he would tear Sam apart, the muscles in his arms bulging, and his brow angry.

Sam laughed, now, but Joseph didn't move his eyes from him.
"I know already," he said. "It was the Judas Tabernacle."

Sam laughed louder.
"But Judas wasn't a Saint," Peter questioned Joseph.

"No," he replied, still watching Sam, "but he was one of the disciples, sent to do the Father's work just as much as Christ was. JAH had to choose one to betray Christ, one who had also heard His Word and walked with His Son."

167

"Let him leave. "Go read your Bible, Sam. We pray for in Peace and Love."

"Wha'! Let him GO! Without a beating!" Peter was astonished.

Joseph just smiled. "Yes. Move you' big self **Peter** and open the door."

We waited while Peter decided whether to follow his own instincts, or obey Joseph. He did both. He opened the door, and then as Sam stepped through, thinking all danger was past, still laughing, he kicked him in his bottom....hard.

Sam's laugh stopped as he hit the ground at the foot of the stairs.

*   *   *   *.

It was four days before Busha arrived. He was finishing a music video in Rio starring a Brazilian singer, and the cost of him leaving the production was greater than the necessity to be with Joseph.

It was strawberry season in England, and in the weeks we spent at Windsor, I grew to love those fruits, which the servants brought to us in so many ways: strawberry fruit salad with oranges, strawberries with thick cream, strawberry pies, and even strawberry juice.

As we sat in front of the TV one afternoon, watching a documentary on African animals, Joseph echoed our thoughts when he said:

"I was just thinking of how far we are now from the dirt floors and macca trees of Wareika, from the days when we use to wish we had something more than cornmeal porridge for our dinner...to now when we are sitting here with white servants bringing us all the fresh fruit we can eat. Bwoy....we are really a special family, you know."

We were indeed; we looked around at each other: Joseph, Mikey, Peter, Red Dread and I. A special people whom JAH had allowed to taste the sweetness of life equal to the bitterness. We had a special responsibility to use our experiences for something important.

Joseph was a man who had realized this long ago, and had acted. The rest of us realized it but had not yet taken the actions we had been sent here to perform.

Each of us, our own Christ, said the Christ.

Joseph, fulfilling his destiny.

When would I fulfill mine? I wondered if the seed in my womb had met life, sprouted, taken hold. I prayed it had, so that I could fulfill a part of my destiny-- to mother a child.

Busha arrived, tanned and glad to be having a rest of sorts. He brought part of his video film crew with him, including the singer, and they took over another wing of the mansion. Thus Busha could work on two things at once, his favourite activity.
And we could use the film epuipment, computers and specialists whom Busha had within reach of his ever present telephone.

Also arriving with Busha, was Suzie, who gave Joseph a friendly hug.

"What a lying bitch that hotel receptionist is, eh?" she smilingly remarked to Joseph, commenting on the headlines. "I know from personal experience that you don't 'eat white meat'.

She laughingly referred to the fact that Joseph did not have sex with non-African blooded women, saying that if the woman bore a child for him, he wanted the child to know itself as fully Black. Then, as Joseph lowered his eyes with a smile, she teased him still further.

"Such a pity. Sure you won't change your mind? My offer is still good!"

Joseph blushed a little, smiling, but suddenly I had an idea. "Would you be prepared to say that on record?" I asked her. "It would help Joseph a lot."

"True confessions? You mean admit it on video that Joseph Planter did not fancy me? Mmm....what a giggle....how funny...well, why not. At least I'd show the quality of what Joseph already refused. He wouldn't be desperate enough to want that little tramp. Sure, I'll do it. The exposure will be good for my career."

And she stretched out her 5 foot eleven inches frame, displaying her Hollywood proportions, and left smiling, saying, "Call me when your ready...."

It took four days to make the international TV and satellite hookups, but using Bush's connections in New York, Los Angeles, London and Jamaica, it was finally announced after ten days that Joseph Planter would address the media, his critics and his fans at a concert to be televised live from Albert Hall in London.

Some media protested, demanded one-on-one interviews, cried down the concert as a media hype event, even demanded that questions be asked in Parliament about the use of such a prestigious venue for the show. In the long run, Tropic's PR people convinced all concerned that Joseph's health would only allow him this one chance to do everything at once.

*   *   *   *

The Albert Hall is located in one of London's prettiest neighbourhoods, Knightsbridge, where the rich people live. It also is opposite to London's most beautiful Park, and in London, the parks are really beautiful.

This Hyde Park is large and full of trees and beautiful, soft-looking grass, and little lakes and ponds, and walkways, and flowering beds, and little bandstands. People run there and nannies walk babies in expensive prams there, and lovers lie on the grass and kiss there, and business men walk to and from

JOSEPH - A RASTA REGGAE FABLE

appointments through there, and Rastafari such as I simply satta there when the sun shines, and enjoy being in such a different but no less beautiful part of JAH creation.

Looking at it from the Park the Albert Hall appears like an enormous wedding cake, with reddish brown icing, edged with white decorations of curls, turrets, domes, statuettes, and all the beauty the architect could place on this monument to the performing arts.

It is round in shape, with entrances all around. Inside it is a high domed palace, with rows of seats on the floors and rising around the sides in tiers are boxes of red velvet covered seats, and higher up, boxes that can hold eight or ten people.

The seats on the downstairs floor had been removed for Joseph's concert, and for the three days before it, I spent a lot of time watching them make preparations, bringing in equipment. That was when I wasn't sitting on a lawn somewhere in Hyde Park.

By the day of the show, the Park was full of hippy and punk types of youths, lots of young black kids, Joseph's fans getting ready for the show. By dusk, the area around the Albert Hall was jammed with cars and people trying to get in, trying to buy tickets, selling red-gold-and green things, spiritual books, African articles.

There were also a growing group of anti-Joseph people, held behind a barrier across the road from the Albert Hall. They had "Keep Britain White" banners, and some of the boys wore Nazi symbols and uniforms. But they were far outnumbered by the people who had been prepared to pay for tickets to Joseph's only British show in three years.

The press, of course was there. Some of it cordoned off behind a PRESS barrier, from behind which they took photos of celebrities arriving in limousines for the show. There were quite a few of those, the trendy rich pop and movie stars who knew enough about the world to know that reggae was 'hot'.

171

Inside, the press also had a section, and this is why the whole of downstairs was needed. Armchair seating had been placed in front of the stage for 100 journalists, their film cameras, tape recorders, and live transmitting equipment. There was also a hospitality table of food and drink for them in a special room in the backstage caverns beside Joseph's dressing room.

The show was, after all for the media more than even the fans.

The stage had been set under a seven foot video screen, which was itself encircled by symbols of Rastafari, crowned at the top with a portrait of the Emperor wearing his coronation Robes and Crown. To one side of the screen was a bank of computer equipment, with two video monitors, while on the other side the sound and lighting controls also included tape and disc playback facilities.

The stage was decorated like a tropical island, and part of the staging was Joseph's idea that his friends and 'family' who had worked to make the show happen, should sit on the stage set and enjoy the show from there. It made the stage seem more friendly, made the show seem more like a family gathering.

Most of all, it gave Joseph some company, rather than the complete aloneness with which he had been expected to face the world's press.

So, Joseph gave his fans a show. A great show....one of his best. Sang his four Number One hits and the fans loved it. But it was not the show we were all there for. It was the encounter with the press. So, striking the strings on his guitar in one unfinished chord and placing it on a rest beside his stool, he took a seat and with the cordless mic in his hand, said:

"Okay, brethren and sistren of the media. Did you enjoy the music?"

The crowd shouted 'yay' and 'more' and clapped, while some of the press grinned sheepishly, or clapped with meaning, or simply sat and waited.

Joseph smiled.
"Well I hope you will enjoy my words as much."

The group of journalists roused themselves. This is what they had come for. Above their heads, on the giant screen flashed the face of Joseph smiling.

"Now tell me why I have been put on trial," Joseph began.
The reporters spluttered, murmured among themselves, annoyed.

"Not a trial, Mr Planter. An interview, a press conference." Larry King of CNN tried to explain.

"Not so," replied Joseph. "What is the real reason for this gathering of journalists? Simply to see if you or someone can make me confess to....to what? To throwing a wild party (which I did not) which got out of hand (which it did not) and therefore I am some sort of moral leper? (Which I am not). If I were a white pop star, or even an aristocratic playboy, or a popular footballer, you wouldn't have bothered to even mention it in your gossip columns." The journalists rustled.

"No, it's what I represent, that has you all angry that you want to hit back at me as powerfully as you can, through the media..." (Joseph held up his hand as the journalists started to protest again)... "but before you all ask me one question, let me ask you all: do you know anything at all about how Black people like me think...WHAT we think?"

He looked around the press section. One journalist put up his hand and said: "Of course we know about Rastafari..." Joseph cut him short.
"I didn't ask you what you know about Rastafari. I asked you if you know how and what we think."

He looked around the press section again, this time he brought his eyes to rest directly on Sam, who was sitting near the rear of the group of journalists. But Sam turned away his eyes and said nothing.

"Well gentlemen...brothers and sisters, allow I and I Idren to give you a brief story-- My story-- so that you can have a true foundation on which to question me. To you, we African-minded people are just troublemakers and nonconformists. But there is a reason why we behave the way we do."

As he spoke, Joseph got up and moved over to the side of the studio set and pressed the button on the VCR which was part of a console television, film and sound equipment.

"There's a reason why we behave like caged, wild animals. To tell the truth that is how we feel-- like caged beasts. Why?"

He pressed the PLAY button, and onto a giant TV screen came a picture of a dreadlocksed man standing with his hand resting on a lion by his side, looking out over a fertile valley with mountains in the distance.

Under this picture rose the music of Marcia Griffiths' song:

> *There's a land that I have heard about*
> *So far across the sea*
> *There's a land that I have heard about,*
> *So far across the sea*
> *To live together in my dream land,*
> *Would be like heaven to me....*

As the music played, Joseph spoke. "We African-minded people have a dream of a special place in Africa where all is perfect love, perfect peace and perfect harmony."

The journalists rustled again. Joseph smiled.

"I know it sounds like a crazy, impossible dream, true. But nevertheless, it is the dream of many thousands and hundreds of thousands of Black people. Some call themselves Rastafari, some Garveyites, some Pan-Africanists, some call themselves "conscious" Africans, some just call themselves Black people, but whatever the conscious Black place they are coming from, we all believe that we can build a new city and a new African nation where we can put the best of our talents to work to make the nation as great as other nations."

"You must wonder why should people want to go to Africa with the conditions that Africa is in? There are wars and famine and apartheid...." Joseph asked.

"A lot of people ask us that question," Joseph continued. "But war and famine and apartheid are not all over Africa. For instance, I don't see any war in the documentary films I watch about the wild life of Africa. Like you ever see a TV show about the lions and zebras and dem thing dey in Africa? Well, Africa has lots of beautiful places like that, where there is open land and animals and wilderness and jungle, just like the continent of America was before the Europeans settled it, or like parts of Australia.

"The reason why we think Africa is just one big war zone, is that you journalists only show us Africa when you get called to report a war or famine. You hardly ever go there to report cultural festival, or a good harvest or an African feature film being made. So the general public which can only get their information about Africa from the media, thinks that there is nothing in Africa except starving babies and gunshots. But like I said, 'there's a land that I have heard about...' and it is ready and waiting for us to go there and populate it." He sat on a high stool.

"So ask me a question now." Joseph demanded.

Larry King cleared his throat and began.
"This land you're speaking about... is this place called Shashemane?"

"Well, yes and no. First, let me show you what Shashemane is like."

He returned to the computer keyboard and punched some keys, and on the screen began the 8mm video film which we had been shooting while in Ethiopia. The beautiful views came on the screen-- a wide field of golden taff waving its shimmering tips in gentle breezes-- all tall guango tree on a hilltop, under which two children played-- a stroll through the forests nearby and the view from a hilltop towards the valley of Shashemane.

Joseph spoke. "Shashemane is a place we love. The Emperor gave it to the Black people of the world who came to the moral and spiritual assistance of Ethiopia during the Italian war. This possession has never been disputed by even the present government, so we are assured of a location for our future city.

"We want to develop it with the small resources we have. But I will admit to you that Shashemane has problems. One of the things we will have to sort out, is the several groups and organizations claim the right to settle the land and lead any development there."

"What would you do to resolve this situation-- I've heard about it," one journalist said.

"Well, said Joseph, "those same groups have so far been unable to do just what they claim the right to, namely: settle and develop. They have only been able to rule, and even so over only a few, so it seems to me that they have already shown themselves unqualified for leadership."

There was a pause. Then another journalist said: "How would YOU establish the nation?" and laughed.

Joseph was serious. He replied.
"When the economic basis for repatriation is established, and the vision becomes a real possibility, leaders will emerge from among the various groups and individuals who genuinely follow the dream. We do not need one leader, but several. We need leaders in many fields to run our ministries, our organizations, even our spiritual observations. These leaders will emerge from a natural movement within the people making the journey, and as the democratic process evolves in our nation, new leaders will have the opportunity to come forth also. No one man can rule this."

"So you don't plan to be the President of this 'kingdom'?" another journalist laughed.

Joseph smiled.

"No, mi bredda. The only plan I have is to be there, for it won't be a 'king-dumb' but a "king-speaks.""

Joseph saw the journalist jump back as his mind received the sounds of Joseph's wordical changes.

A woman dressed in khaki stuck up her hand. "What would you do there....farm?"

Joseph leaned back.
"Well I personally would make music. That is my work. I would set up a recording studio there and make my albums there. And I guess my brethren who are doctors would run the hospitals, and my sisters who are teachers would educate the children, and the farmers would grow food for us and perhaps even for export, and the carpenters and masons would build the residences and business places, and the craftsmen would bring beauty to our lives."

The journalist smiled. Joseph continued. "In fact, one of the busiest set of brethren, I believe, will be our travel agents booking trips for people like you to come and see our beautiful country."

The journalist smiled back, and then took notes on her pad, while another hand shot up and King took the question.

The journalist waited till the buzz had died down in the studio, to put his question in a cool and deadly voice.
"I understand you expect me, and the American and European journalists here, and the Americans and Europeans watching this....this media hype of a Jim Jones-type cult which worships a dead despot and hates white people....you expect us to finance this pipe dream."

The camera closed up on a face that was smooth pink, balding, and tightlipped. His on-screen name ID features were blonde, blue-eyed and fined nosed. You could see that he was expecting Joseph to get angry.

"Sir." Joseph spoke strongly. "Some thirty years ago, the people of a certain faith were given the right to establish a nation of their own in the north of Africa. The religion they followed was not popular in the world, especially since this religion did not worship God in the same way most Christians did. Nevertheless, on moral grounds, the right of this religion and this people to form a nation to live together was so strong, that they received it, and today they are fighting every day to retain this hard-fought-for right." Joseph's voice was calm.

"That of course was the state of Israel, and the people of many nations have paid the costs of establishing and maintaining that nation.   Now, sir although you do not have a correct interpretation of my own beliefs as a Rastafari, you cannot question my human right to think and act and worship as I do.

"Apart from that, I want to emphasize that it is not just Rastafari who want to create this new African nation. It is Black people all over the world, Rasta and non-Rasta, Pan Africanists, Garveyites, Muslims, Anglicans, Protestants, no-church...the only thing that unities us is our Blackness and our desire for repatriation.

"Now let me deal with the part of your question regarding money and who will pay. You, sir, are paying right now the cost of your forefather's enslavement of the Blackman and woman. You are paying in riots in your ghetto's, drugs on your streets, unemployment, poor housing, violence, murder, crowded prisons, dangerous streets....you are paying a heavy cost in those countries which were built on the profits of slavery.

"You are paying again when you have to send food and monetary aid to assist the countries that were created as slave plantations, factories for creating wealth to build your nations. Your countries spend billions of dollars a year on these costs.

Now think what a wise investment it might be, if your countries were to invest a small percentage of this expenditure on letting some of your unwanted Black people set up a "company" let us say, that might help to reduce this costly expenditure of yours? I think this sounds like good economic sense, don't you?"

"How much, per capital do you estimate it will cost?" the journalist continued, his lips still tight.

"That is something that will have to be worked out in discussion and negotiation, based on precedence which has been set in the case of Israel, and other peoples who have repatriated in various ways and for various reasons from other countries. I couldn't give you a figure."

(We, watching, were surprised at Joseph's denial that he did not know the possible cost, for this was one of the figures we had worked out, and the information was on the computer.)

"How much do you think would be a fair figure to award such a returning resident who wishes to set up home and assist in the development of a nation?" Joseph leaned his head on the side, with that little smile of his. The journalist battled back.

"Perhaps the best way would be just to decide on a lump sum and donate it to the Rastafari movement."

Joseph shook his head.
"That would present a whole heap of problems."

"Like...who would receive that sum? And in the name of who? And who would decide how it should be shared up?

"No.

"The only way is for each person who wants to be repatriated to receive a certain sum of money, and a portion for each member of his family. Then each family or individual would decide where they would invest this money, in what country, with what groups of people, etc.

"What I would hope is that most people would decide to pool the money communally, saving back a portion for their own personal use and pooling the rest into a big fund which our financial brains could invest to bring the best return with which to build a city and nation. We have worked out some costs for building basic infrastructure-- residences, services etc for a city of about 100,000 persons using each modern building methods and technology. We can give you a breakdown of costs in each sector. All of these costs and plans are contained in this document."

He held in his hand a brightly coloured book bearing the same picture of a man and a lion against a background of a beautiful countryside view.

"What sort of city do you have in mind?" Have you thought about it also?" a journalist in the top row asked.

Joseph turned again to the computer and pressed a key. The computer activated a programme using computer graphics and commentary which created a guided tour of the city of the future.

"Welcome to New Zion-- Africa's newest nation. Our city is designed by the finest Black architects, using modern technology combined with the principles of Ancient Africa-- of Egypt, of Timbuktoo, of Mali, of Songhai, of Ghana and of Axum.

Our city is centered around the Temple of the Twelve Saints. This temple is twelve sided around a central altar, and is a large enough to comfortably hold 50,000 worshippers.

Around the temple are the residences for the twelve priests of the Temple, representing the Twelve Tribes of Israel and Twelve Mansions of Black Christhood."

"What are they?" asked another journalist.

"Some of them are Nyabingi, Boboshanti, Twelve Tribes,

Ethiopian World Federation, but some of the names are known only those to who celebrate the Black Christhood, and must not be revealed lightly."

Joseph released the PAUSE button and the videotape continued.

"Around the residences of the Priests is the circle of residences of the Ministers of State. There will be Twelve Ministers governing the affairs of the nation. The first and most important of these will be the Theological Law, which will govern the rules and practices of the nation and its people. It will be a theocratic law, and its interpretation will be strictly based on the scriptures and holy books of African antiquity.

"Other Ministries will be Women and Children, which will include Education."

"How will you select the Ministers?" one asked.

"Temporary leaders will be selected in the initial years, whose skills are known already; but the building process will show up new leaders and democratic systems will place them in position. This will be the work of the community groups."

"Each of the twelve sectors of the city will contain a primary, secondary and tertiary institution, as pre-primary education will be the responsibility of parents at home. Schools in each sector will aspire to develop skills appropriate to the sector, thus students can move between schools, as well as opt to remain in school in their own sector.

"Housing will be a priority ministry, with employees for this sector being recruited first for repatriation. As well as architects, builders, carpenters, masons, plumbers and so on will be needed first to develop the city. Workers in this sector will receive houses first, and will be allowed to take time off from work to work on their own residences. Housing in the city will be developed along the line of apartment blocks and estates grouped together in walled off sectors each with their own green spaces and community facilities. It will be the duty of residents to develop community groups and industries for the improvement of the nation.

"The Health Ministry will operate medical services in each sector, located in the circle around the housing circle.

"Industry will develop all aspects of manufacturing including mining, assembly and production of goods, processing of agricultural products, and its related offices and services. With this Ministry located so near to the residential area, and with access through the health circle, not only will travel to and from work be fairly easy to accomplish, but also there will be the constant reminder to the community of the need to assist in caring for its sick and aged.

"The Economics Ministry will run the finances of the nation, in all its aspects including billing, imports and exports, taxation if necessary, and so on.

"We want to have a Science Ministry to give special attention to the technology of the 21st century and the discoveries we feel will surely come out of such a favourable environment.

"We will have a Ministry of the Creative Arts, to look after the music and film studios we will build, the publishing houses, the satellite dish stations, and the plastic arts we will create.

"We will need a Ministry for Energy and one for Transportation.

"Finally, we will circle the city with two broad bands. The first will be for recreation, which will have its own Ministry. This will include tourism, amusement parks, campsites-- things of that nature. Next to Recreation will be Agriculture Circle, which will be the largest band of all, where we will farm the food needed for the nation. The borders of this circle are endless, as are its agrarian possibilities. Between the recreation and Agricultural Circles will be a circle of housing for visitors and agricultural workers.

"Each sector of the city o New Zion will be designated a colour, and residents and workers of each sector will strive to decorate and beautify their sector according to the sector colours-- thus creating a magically coloured rainbow city."

On the screen appeared a view of the city, spread out flat as if seen from the sky above. Each of the twelve spokes of the design were coloured with one of the Twelve Priests colours and closeups zoomed into hanging brackets of blue plumbago dripping over apartment walls in the blue sector, or vines laden with peaches in the peach-coloured sector. Red woven hammocks swung from the limbs of scarlet poinsettia trees in the red sector, while shades of sand, brown and beige enhanced the stark whites of the sectors whitewashed walls. Purple grapes and bouganvillea flourished in one sector, while in another householders had created a giant water habitat for their favourite birds, flamingoes.

The videographical tour of the mythical city ended with a focus on the Black Madonna and Child resting under the velvet, gold-braided hangings of the Temple's altar.

"Well, hope you enjoyed the trip." Joseph smiled.

There was a little silence when the screens images faded. Then Larry King said: "I see you have given the matter a great deal of thought, Joseph."

"Not just me, Larry. A lot of good minds have gone into this presentation. What I think the Repatriation Movement has been lacking for a long time, is a really well-presented document about the issue. No one or group has really sat down and made up a set of facts to present out case.

"So I got in touch with some of the brothers and sisters who felt I could really help create a nation if we got a chance, and this is what we came up with. It's not really fine-tuned yet, but at least its a working document. What do you think of it?"

King leaned back, rubbed his chin and smiled.

"It's kinda nice. I'd like to live there myself. Can I apply for residency?" He laughed.

Joseph was serious.

"Much as I'd like to be able to say yes, Larry, you've got to admit that first option on living there should go to descendants of African slavery. You know, you've raised an important point, Larry. There are some people who are not Black, but claim Rasta as their faith. They wear locks, live a red-green-and gold life, and some of them are even married to Black people, to Rastas. They feel they have a right to repatriation if it comes. Bit I personally believe that they will have to wait until every son and daughter of Africa comes home first. Don't you agree, Larry?"

King paused for a moment. "Well, I've got to agree that the word 'repatriation' implies returning to a place you come from. At any rate, the vacation accommodation looks fine to me. But Joseph, you could afford the fare. Why don't you just go back to Africa?" King asked.

"It's not just for me, that I am asking, Larry. It is for all of us. We can't build a city with ten people. We need hundreds, thousands, millions of people, just like the State of Israel." Joseph replied.

Before he could say more, a hand shot up from the back of the studio. It was Sam, shouting.

"Joseph, you are here to answer the charge that your music and behaviour are corrupting the morals of the society which you hope will buy your records. What you are giving us here is an excuse for your behaviour."

Joseph turned slowly to face Sam, and looked him in the eyes long before speaking.

"Brethren and sistren, may I introduce you to Brother Sam Bergman, the journalist who travelled with us to Ethiopia, and indeed the journalist who was with us in our hotel suite on the night when the alleged 'wild party' took place. Sam, my brother, maybe you can give your fellow journalists a true account of that evening."

"It's all true," Sam shouted. "And nothing this little tramp can say, can change it." He held up a copy of the previous day's DAILY MIRROR, on whose front page was a photo interview with Suzie: "I LIVED WITH JOSEPH ON A DESERT ISLAND AND HE NEVER TOUCHED ME! Once again the truth had been perverted to maintain the lie.

Joseph was serious now.
"Sam, you more than anyone else here, should know that what I'm presenting tonight is the real answer to any problem that I, or my music, or my beliefs, present to your world. And I truly believe that if you, or any persons in your world, are offended by my lifestyle or my very existence in your world, then the best thing you can do is ship me out of your world to the world that I claim is mine." Sam started shouting him down, but Joseph continued.

"If you really want to be fair about it, you should pay the costs of returning us to Africa to help erase the terrible crimes of slavery that your ancestors inflicted on our people three hundred and more years ago. For remember, the Book of Jeremiah says:
"Woe unto him that buildeth his house by unrighteousness, and his chambers by wrong; that useth his neighbours services without wages, and giveth him not for his work."

"And Sam, I believe that you, who have shared so much with us as a white man, should be able to tell your fellow white men the truth about what we believe-- not help to destroy us who took you in and trusted you, even though you are white."

Sam's laughter burst through his anger.
"Don't quote damn scripture at me, boy. And, for your information, I AM NOT WHITE."

The bombshell hit us as hard as it showed on Joseph's face.

185

"I'm as black as you," Sam continued. "The black son of a Jewish father and a Jamaican maid who used to clean his house. Unfortunately, I came out looking like my father, but I had to grow up in the slums of Chicago....where the little black kids used to taunt me and call me Jewboy, until I vowed I would get my revenge, especially on you half-breeds who have the luck to be born with black skin!" He was scowling with rage.

"And if I have been able to expose the number one black hero of the world as nothing more than a sex-crazed drug addict who worships a dead dictator, and all this..." his hand swept across the auditorium "..as nothing more than a giant public relations attempt to whitewash your immorality, then I feel maybe there's some justice in the world."

There was a buzz of unease in the crowd, and several journalists tried to get in questions of their own, but Sam would not let up.

"Ask him about his wife. Ask him! Why do we never hear you speak of your wife? Are you married or not?" Sam shouted across the noise.

Joseph waited until the noise subsided, as he knew it would to hear his answer. His head flopped down on his chest, and finally raised it slowly and looked at Sam, then over to us, then back at Sam.

"You really want my blood and guts tonight, don't you?" then he raised his eyes to the wider crowd and said: "Brethren and sistren, I am married to a woman who is not interested in having sex." And he spread his hands wide, in a gesture that needed no further explanation. "I did not intend that this should be the place for such a revelation, which is why I keep my sex life private, or try to."

There was a pause, but Sam was not finished yet.

"And what about Jews, Joseph? I dare you to deny you hate Jews!"

You could have heard that pin drop they always speak about, it went so quiet in that large, large Albert Hall.

Joseph shook his head, a little sadly, and got down off the stool. He stood there, bathed in the spotlight.

"Sam, you asked me that question once before, but you never waited for an answer. I'm glad you gave me a chance to answer it in front of so many people, so you won't be able to misquote me, ever again."

"I am a Rastafari lion of the tribe of Judah, one of the tribes of Israel. If you read in First Kings, Chapter Eleven verse 31, you will read of what JAH said: *"Behold I will rend the Kingdom out of the land of Solomon, and give ten tribes to thee; But ye shall have one tribe for my servant David's sake, the city which I have chosen out of all the tribes of Israel."*

"I and I are that one tribe. They call I & I Falasha Jews. That means that all the people of the other tribes of Israel are I & I brethren. The Jews use the same Biblical laws as I, the same Psalms; they believe in the forthcoming of the Christ as prophesied by the Prophet Isaiah. So, while I may not agree with how the Jews are defending the land they have been given to dwell in, still I have to find common cause with them because of this spiritual bond."

"Then again, the Jews of Israel have set the precedent of repatriation with reparations, so again I look to them as a kind of elder brethren going in the right direction. Their system of living and working together, kibutzim, is in harmony with African ways. I really have no problem with the Jewish people," Joseph raised his shoulders.

"As to their wealth and control of nations, here again I see a people who can teach I & I a great deal, a people with whom we Africans will continue to trade our gold and diamonds when the African majority has political control of these resources."

"So why should you think that I & I harbour hatred for any

group of persons, anywhere in the world? What I & I hate is evil, and let me tell you... you find evil EVERYWHERE, in Jews and Christians, in Rastafari and Muslim. Because until JAH Kingdom come on earth, Satan will rule and the world will see more evil than good."

He paused, then continued: "You, Sam are some of that evil."

"You little shit," Sam snarled, gathering up his notebooks an tape recorder to leave. "What have YOU ever done to get your people 'home'?"

"I was just coming to that, Sam." It stopped Sam in his tracks, but Joseph had already turned to signal me, and then back to his audience. The tape pressed flashed a Bank Statement and Account Number on the screens, noting a deposit of Five Million US Dollars to open: THE ETHIOPIAN REPATRIATION FUND.

"Yes, me brethren, I decided to put my money where my mouth is, and I have started the ball rolling. Now the account is open: it is open to governments whose consciences lead them in this direction, and it is open to individuals who feel they can make a contribution. Those who wish can make their contribution in labour, giving of their skills to help in the repatriation and building, and will be credited according to the going rate of their particular skill. I also livicate the royalties for eternity of I song "*LOVE ALL*" to the Fund.

With that, he put down the mic, picked up his guitar and signalled the band to start the chords of his most popular song.

The audience rose its feet clapping and singing the familiar tune and words, rocking happily, enjoying the closing moments of what had certainly been an event to talk about. Journalists started leaving, but the audience stayed, even as Joseph left the stage, was called back by their shouts, left again, returned and finally, with arms outstretched shouted one last

JAH

and the crowd responded

RASTAFARI!

And he could finally escape, exhausted, from it all.

As he fell back against the cushions of the blue van, I could see by the pain on his forehead that his wound was still hurting him.

He was sicker than we knew. He was dying.

CHAPTER TWELVE

"Blessed are the meek; for they shall inherit the earth. Blessed are they which hunger and thirst after righteousness, for they shall be filled. Blessed are the pure in heart; for they shall see God (JAH). Blessed are they which are persecuted for righteousness' sake: for theirs is the Kingdom of Heaven.
GOSPEL OF ST. MATTHEW; CHAPTER 5: Vs. 5, 6, 8, 9.

There's not much else of Joseph's story you don't know.

You know how he collapsed when we got back at the hotel from the concert that was more a press conference. You know the rest, because it was world news for days after...the concert, the press conference, and Joseph's illness.

He just spurted up some blood, and then fell over on the sofa in the hotel suite.

The Tropic people had called Busha's private doctor, who rushed him to the intensive care unit of one of London's private medical facilities, where the doctors asked to operate immediately.

"No," Joseph insisted, weakly. "I want I & I bush doctors. No others must touch me."

Mikey found a Sons of Jacob brother in London... The Doc, as he was always called... a Rastafarian brother who had studied and become a medical doctor after first learning all the herbal healing he could from his Nyabingi father.

The Doc made his examination, quietly and thoroughly, using not only his traditional methods, but adding a special method of diagnosing using a silver rod to tune into vital organs and points. He spent a lot of time sounding Joseph's chest, then he covered him up and stepped into the outer room where we waited.

"Joseph has a lesion in his chest... a tumor. Apparently, where the broken rib stuck into the flesh around it, a tumor has formed instead of healing, and the pus in that place is terrible. I am amazed he has not collapsed before now."

Busha sat down, put his head in his hands and wept. Suzie put her arms around him comfortingly, and she too wept on his bowed shoulder. I went over and sat beside them, patting Suzie, saying 'hush', but the weeping was contagious and I too was crying.

"How are you going to treat him?" Busha asked our question. He was as worried as we, and not just because of his investment. Joseph was his friend too, the piece of him that was rooted in the Jamaican soil. He could not think of life without Joseph's friendship.

"Well, first of all, we must get him back to Jamaica," The Doc said seriously. "That's the first step in his treatment."
Busha nodded.

"Then we need a quiet place away from everything....somewhere clean and quiet with good vibrations. No people. Then I will begin the physical treatments, and the place I have in mind offers the best."

"But why do we have to move him so far?" Busha asked. "There are good places in Europe...health spas....there's a good one in Italy..."

The Doc cleared his throat.

"Yes, and there's the Debre Zeit Monastery in Jamaica. THAT'S where I want him, if we are to save him."

We flew by private jet to Jamaica, then by helicopter to Debre Zeit, the hillside monastery where the Nyabingi elders who kept themselves away from Babylon live in prayer, fasting and meditation. There we began Joseph's treatment.

191

I know you read in the media and saw the TV interviews, that assured you that The Doc and the elders and all of us did everything we possibly could, to save Joseph's life.

But I don't think you know how hard we really tried, and just how and what we tried, to save the life of our dear Brother Joseph. I can tell you of the high enemas to flush out the poisons from his system, the teas, the hot and cold baths, the juices, the herbs, the gently prepared food.

And the prayers. Debre Zeit Monastery is at the top of a range mountains in the St. Andrew Hills. Access is by a one hour climb up an unmarked mountain track wide enough only to place a foot, with a precipice below and rocks above. At times the river rushes below, making waterfalls and dangerous crossings over large stones. But it is because it is so inaccessible, that it is beloved by those members of the Rastafari faith who want to rest, mediate and perhaps take on priestly vows; a place where Nyabingi and Church become one, as it was in the beginning.

Life here is rudimentary...wattle huts, carry water, hardly a hillside to plant food on, and the river strength sometimes low. But quiet and peaceful, away from mankind, high up in the clouds nearest to JAH. At Debre Zeit, the only human noise allowed is the sound of prayer.

Few people make the climb, for it is terrible and exhausting, only for the fit in body and heart.

There, we were given the largest dwellings in which we all camped, while the Doc transformed one larger house into Joseph's treatment room, getting them to bring up special beds and cloths and medical items, whitewashing the walls and floor, and putting in two cots for himself and the dread who was his assistant.

Yes, I know you know all about that, because there wasn't a world news media that didn't carry the stories about Joseph, as his health grew worse.

I know you also read about the first donations to the Repatriation Fund from that group of rock and roll superstars, and you probably bought a copy of the record and video they made in support, which put 14 million US Dollars into our fund.

I am quite sure you did not miss hearing about the gift of the Government and people of that repatriated State. Wasn't it incredible!

To give One Billion Dollars out of the Three Billion they receive from the US each year, was wonderful enough.

But better still, were the words of the Foreign Minister. Remember? He said: "The children of our State acknowledge the existence of a branch of the Tribe of Judah, namely Ethiopians, and support their efforts to be restored to the land of their fathers. While we will continue to defend the right of our nation to exist, we believe that repatriation and reparations are not the exclusive rights of any race, people or religion."

I was absolutely astonished.
JAH is amazing, isn't He?

I know that you know that England is having problems with the numbers of people who have applied for Repatriation with Reparations. I read about the demonstrations too.

All I have to say, is that Joseph would say: "Everybody jus' cool. Everything will work itself out soon; money will come and a way will be found. Prepare well for the step you want to take, and don't mash up your chances yet, for JAH loves a patient soul." That's what Joseph would say, I know it.

I read that article that journalist wrote, saying that Joseph's life was a struggle between the Ethiopian Orthodox Church and the Nyabingi Order, and that neither side won.

But that is an incorrect analysis. Once when Mikey asked him if he felt the trip to Ethiopia was to prove that the Church was the best part of Rastafari, Joseph said:

"No, it's not that. The Church, like every other Church, is full of people, and people are just people, whether they have locks or say JAH or not. In fact, a lot of what people do in church, could want to put other people off from joining the Church, just like every other Church, even Rasta."

"But what the Ethiopian Church has, are the prayers. To me, the Prayers of the Ethiopian Church are the most beautiful and the most powerful. That is the secret strength the Ethiopian Orthodox Church give I & I Rastafari, and we would be foolish not to use this beauty and power to reach our destiny." He wasn't finished.

"The next thing about the Ethiopian Church, is that while Rastafari is not recognized worldwide, the Church is. The Church can even petition the United Nations. So just at a wordly level, it is good for I & I to be apart of such an organization, because it can be the vehicle to take us back to worship with our fellow Ethiopians, in our ancient cathedrals, temples and holy shrines."

"Hey, did you know there's an Ethiopian Church and monastery in Jerusalem? Yeah! And it's not the only one in Israel, either; and there's even some in Egypt."

"You know man, when I think about living in Africa, I think about when my children come and ask me to send them on holidays, I can send them to Jerusalem, or to see the Pyramids in Egypt, or in a safari in Kenya, or to hear a rock concert in Johannesburg. Instead of just Miami and New York, and Babylon. When I&I travel Africa through the Church, our journey will be RASpected."

"But at the same time, I&I are the Nyabingi Order of the Church, and when we arrive in Ethiopia we will be already known by our dreadlocks, which in Ethiopia are the mark of the priests. I&I Melchizedek Order is holy and upright, full of the Christ Light which we received through Selassie I, JAH RASTAFARI."

194

That was Joseph's answer, so instead of a battle lost, a victory of unity was won by Joseph's life.

You're probably wondering about Rosy and Zuelika.

Of course, we let Rosy know where Joseph was, and arranged for her to see him. After all, she was his wife, and the mother of one of his children.

The joys of having enough food to eat all the time, at last, rested amply on Rosy's body. She came puffing up the hill with a group of three other woman friends. Two of them were not dressed properly to pass the Middle Gate of Strength on the mountain track, the Gate beyond which only those mindful that they were entering a holy place, may continue. So they had to wait for Rosy at the basic school just below the Middle Gate, while Rosy puffed up the hill. The climb angered her.

"How you mean to bring my husband up to this ungodly place to die? Who give you permission to kill him off?" she demanded of The Doc.

Then seeing Joseph cried out: "Oh Joseph, my beloved husband," and threw herself on him, where he lay on the low bed.

"Oh Joseph; how you mean to tell the world on TV that I don't want you. Is not that I don't want you, is YOU don't want me! "Oh what them do you, bwoy? My God, a-kill them a-kill you! Oh Joseph, speak to me, speak to me."

She sobbed loudly, her arms spread around his shoulders, her body and clothes smothering him, until we heard Joseph's faint voice: "....get her off me, too heavy.."

"Oh, I'm sorry..." she jumped off him, pushing her hand into a pocket and coming out with a hanky in which she blew her nose loudly. Joseph felt his neck weakly.

"My cross...my Ethiopian cross.."

Mikey grabbed Rosy's hand from behind and twisted it painfully. The silver cross Joseph had been given at his baptism, fell from her hand and lay on the ground between us, its points giving off flashes of light.

Rosy bawled and covered her face with her hand. Only her mouth could be seen, sobbing, drooling, as she cried: "He's MY husband....what's his is mine...the magic of the cross must come to me and MY child... I WANT THE CROSS!"

I yanked down her hand from her face, and pushed my own in front of hers. "What magic?" I demanded to know. "Who told you about any magic cross?"

"Sam told me." She spat it out. "Sam told me that Joseph got a special gift in Ethiopia, and he figured it was something to do with the baptism and the cross he got afterwards. So if he is dying, that cross is MINE."

"For heavens sake, woman. There's no magic in that cross. Your husband is dying, and all you are interested in is what you are going to receive after his death! After all you have received already! I can't believe you could be so cold!"
I spoke the truth in my heart.

"Cold? Cold!' Rosie stepped back snarling. "I am as cold as the cold nights I spent going to bed hungry belly, baby crying and no money coming in from my husband. I am as cold as the cold lonely nights I spent, while Joseph was sleeping in another woman's bed. I am as cold as I have been treated by all the people, including you, who flock around Joseph and gave him bad advice, and sucked him out for the money he could make, and are trying to save his life now that he is dying."

"Yes, woman. I am cold. I have a right to be cold. But we'll see who has the last laugh. I will win in the end."

And without a further look at Joseph, she went out of the dwelling, called to her woman friend, and went off down the hill, and out of our lives forever.

Yes, the woman Zuelika, also came up the hill. Found out from Busha where Joseph was, she said, when I went down the Middle Gate to question her. She just wanted to see Joseph; she was begging, pleading. She just wanted to be with him. For a minute, for an hour, for just a glimpse through a window. Anything, she would be grateful for.

I had come back to tell her that the Doctors said Joseph could have no visitors, for they were on a special five day treatment of fasts and baths which needed isolation. Zuelika would have to wait, also, at the basic school.

Surprisingly, but nothing about Zuelika surprised anyone, especially me -- surprisingly, she spent the first day's wait getting involved with the children and the teachers, and after that first day, one of the teachers gave her a sleeping place at her house, and she continued in this way for the five days until Joseph's treatment was finished.

We spent such anxious days and nights at Debre Zeit, thinking about Joseph and what he was suffering. Thinking too, about ourselves. Joseph was the cement that had united us as a family. His energy, his career, his life, was what provided us with energy, career and life, also.

Without Joseph, we were nothing. Just individuals from different walks of life, united only by faith, but unable to survive as a unit, perhaps even as individuals. None of us, except perhaps The Doc, had a house to live in; none of us had an income.

Not that we looked to Joseph for support-- it was just that it had worked out that way. Joseph's delight to be able to afford to have his close friends be with him all the time, had provided for our economic needs. JAH, through Joseph was our supply.

When our reasoning reached that point, we realized that the same JAH that provided, would keep on providing as long as we kept the faith.

Indeed, the same JAH was probably was just putting us through a test of faith right here and now, with Joseph himself.

When the reasoning reached this part, we were hit with determination to endure this time with steel-like spiritual strength, and after we had thought about this intention for a long silence, one by one we each got up, went outside, found a place of quiet meditation, our Bibles, and stayed this way until dusk fell and it was time for supper.

"Let us fast for a day," Mikey suggested at supper. "See what happens, what message JAH sends."

Good idea, we all agreed, so the next day we fasted on prayers and water only. When night fell that day, The Doc said he wanted to try one final treatment which he had only heard of from an elder, long, long ago, and which he did not really believe could work. It was the process used for preserving the bodies of dead Egyptians, and he wanted to try to use it on Joseph before he was actually dead.

It consisted of plastering the body with the flesh of red-ripe aloes, then wrapping it in a gauze soaked in myrrh, frankincense and herbs, then administering heat and light constantly for 36 hours.

He explained this to us, saying that they would screen off a place in the open where Joseph could be laid in the light of the sun during the days. The problem, however, was to know what he could do to retain the heat of the body during the night. If we had electricity, we could put up an infra-red red light, or plug in heaters, but we didn't.

"I think it could work, if body heat was used to substitute. One of us would have to strip off and lie with Joseph during the night hours till dawn, three nights running."

He turned to look around at us, Peter and Mikey, Red Dread, his assistant Ras Esrak.

"It's not going to be a comfortable experience, on many levels," he said to the brethren. "So I will volunteer for the first night. Sister Shanty, we excuse you from duty."

But as he excused me, my idea came.
"Why not give Zuelika the job? I'm sure it's something she would willingly do well, and with no embarrassment."

The brethren looked around them. They knew from my reports that Zuelika was at the Middle Gate, and also about how she had passed her time while waiting.

So it was, that Zuelika got a chance to help keep our beloved Joseph alive. With a screen drawn over a corner of the dwelling, Zuelika spent three nights, warming his nearly lifeless body with her own body warmth and covering herself with nothing more than her golden brown locks.

"Thank you, Ashanti," she whispered to me, before she took her place that first night, after the first day.
"How can I ever thank you?"

"Ask him what was his temple in Ethiopia," I begged her.

She told me the next morning.

"The Ark of the Covenant! That's what he said!

"Ask him tonight what was inside the Ark," I urged her.
"Why?" she asked.

"It's important," was all I could say.

She said that Joseph said that inside the Ark of the Covenant was a great LIGHT.

EPILOGUE

So that's how I come to be writing these few chapters, sitting on a pile of lumber, watching the brethren building more and more new dwellings of our beautiful Shashemane, the Holy City.

Beside me, my little son Johannes is playing with his pieces of wood, trying to be like the brethren already, at just one and a half years old. He looks so much like his father, Peter. JAH is wonderful, and to be praised. Praise is due to the Blessed Mother, Mary, who made intercession for I to Her Son, the Christos, through Her Wonderful Prayer. I give Thanks and Praise.

Johannes was delivered at the medical centre here, built and directed by The Doc. He arrived here when we did, two weeks after Joseph's funeral, when I was five months pregnant, and he helped Peter build our first house.

We Shashemane mothers are teaching our own children, and we have made a big school room with all our teaching equipment and toys. Red Dread's baby mother has a Masters in Education, so we will not be isolated.

As the travel fund is activated, more and more builders, doctors and teachers keep coming, and our city is growing wonderfully.

I am one of the lucky ones, but I knew that right from the start, from the day I met Joseph Planter in my father's backyard at Wareika.

Well, now you know everything. So I can finally put down my pen, and rest my hand.

There's Joseph now, coming to play with Johannes.
Johannes really loves Joseph.

Yes, Joseph.

No. Joseph is not dead. You would hardly recognize him though, without his long locks.

Yes, the treatment worked.

What was buried at his 'funeral' was a wax dummy of him that the San Diego Museum made for an exhibition three years ago, and presented to Joseph when the exhibition was finished.

It had been Joseph's idea.
"Let them think I have died. It's the only way I can live in peace."

We placed the locks in the coffin, beside the wax dummy. It helped to make the 'body' look more real. Without his locks, no one recognized him on his journey from Jamaica to Africa.

Joseph says he wants Zuelika's baby to be a girl, so she can be wife to Johannes. Yes, Zuelika is here with us, also.

We're looking forward to seeing you here soon, to help us build. There's lots of room.

And lots of LOVE.

ASHANTI
Shashemane, Ethiopia.
The Year of St. Matthew, 1977
(1984-85, Western Calender)

THE END

9 781482 678895